Out of the Storm

Masters of the Prairie Winds Club
Book One

by Avery Gale

Copyright © October 2015 by Avery Gale
ISBN 978-1-944472-17-7
All cover art and logo © Copyright 2015 by Avery Gale
All rights reserved.

The Masters of the Prairie Winds Club® and Avery Gale®
are registered trademarks

Cover Design by Jess Buffett
Published by Avery Gale

Thank you for respecting the hard work of this author.

This is a work of fiction. Names, places, characters and incidents either are the product of the author's imagination or are used fictitiously and any resemblance to any actual persons, living or dead, organizations, events or locales are entirely coincidental.

No part of this book may be reproduced, stored in a retrieval system, or transmitted by any means without the written permission of the author and publishing company.

WARNING: The unauthorized reproduction or distribution of this copyrighted work is illegal. Criminal copyright infringement, including infringement without monetary gain, is investigated by the FBI and is punishable by up to 5 years in federal prison and a fine of $250,000.

If you find any books being sold or shared illegally, please contact the author at avery.gale@ymail.com.

Dedication

A huge thanks to Clint and Kimberly Bollinger in Sealy, Texas, for their technical advice and permission to use that great fence on the cover. Oh yes, they are very real and just as helpful and talented in real-life as they are in the book and I can't tell you how much their friendship means to me.

For all the great metalwork described in Out of the Storm or anything else your imagination dares…be sure to contact Clint at www.egafab.com.

Chapter One

Kyle West couldn't remember the last time he'd driven in a worse thunderstorm. The lightning was flashing so close that it was blinding him for a few seconds after each strike and the thunder cracks were jarring his damned teeth. The pounding rain was coming down in sheets and looking as if it was blowing horizontally. It was also falling faster than the water could drain from the black asphalt so his truck was continually right on the verge of hydroplaning. *Damn it, I should have left that meeting when I wanted to. Hell, I'd already be home and changed out of this fucking monkey suit.*

There wasn't much in the world Kyle West hated more than meetings with investors and advertisers that he didn't need or want, or city traffic, and wearing a damned tie. And today he'd had to deal with all of the above and his patience was about as thin as it could get without him going off the deep end. The local weather forecasters had been talking about a chance of sudden cloudbursts, but this was far beyond that lame-assed description if you asked him. Kyle had decided years ago that forecasting the weather anywhere in the central part of the United States had to involve a monkey on crack in the backroom of the television station with a quarter for flippin'. He'd seen all those fancy storm chaser vans racing around the countryside the past few years, but he hadn't noticed the forecasts getting any more accurate. Yep, a monkey and a coin could probably save the taxpayers millions.

Pressing the button to connect to his hands-free phone, he wasn't surprised when he got the automated message saying he didn't have any wireless service. Hell, service out in the boonies of Texas hill country could be spotty on a sunny day and with this kind of torrential storm, he would have been more surprised if he'd *had* service. Kyle wanted to call the club and let them know he was only about an hour out, but it didn't look like that was going to happen. Hopefully their housekeeper had left him something to eat because he hadn't wanted to stop in Austin before heading home.

His brother, Kent, was going to owe him big for this one, yes indeed. Usually his twin went to these meetings and rubbed elbows with the rich, famous, and annoying. But Kent had promised to help a couple of their buddies settle into one of the cabins that had been fixed up behind the club. Both Ash and Dex had been on their SEAL team, and when the pair of Doms decided they weren't going to re-up, Kyle and Kent hadn't wasted any time signing them on as security and Dungeon Monitors.

After talking to owners of other BDSM clubs all over the globe, they'd decided to avoid volunteer dungeon monitors and instructors if possible. Their membership fees were high enough that it would easily cover the salaries of trained personnel. Both he and Kent wanted to do everything they could to make the club a model for safe, sane, and consensual play, and having experienced staff was essential to meeting that goal. The safety of each one of their members would always be their number one priority and every decision they made was to that end.

When he and Kent had first started scouting locations

for the club they'd envisioned, real estate agents had shown them every piece of shit warehouse their companies had listed. Most of the buildings they had looked at would have needed to be completely razed and rebuilt in order to meet safety codes. However, a casual conversation with a fellow Dom led them to the perfect property. The Dom was one of the few commercial bankers Kyle had ever met that he thought actually had a conscience. The man was in the process of closing down a middle-aged couple's dream project because they'd fallen victim to the economic downturn that had turned the average person's vacation money into gas and grocery funds. Kent and Kyle had expressed an interest when he'd described the property and he'd set up a meeting for the next day. When they'd met Don and Patty Reynolds, both he and Kent had liked the couple immediately and it had been easy to see why the banker had felt so bad about pulling the plug on the dude ranch and retreat center the Reynolds had been building.

It was instantly apparent that Don Reynolds was a Dom and that his lovely wife was his submissive. When he and Kent explained their plans for the property, both had eagerly asked if there was any chance they could stay on as employees and the West brothers had hired them on the spot. Don had proven to be an amazing carpenter, mechanic, and landscaper. His lovely wife, Patty, was working as their housekeeper and cook even though her cooking *expertise* was something of a running joke. Kyle chuckled to himself thinking back on all the times they had all eaten absolutely horrible food simply because no one had wanted to hurt her feelings. Kyle was glad that Ash and Dex were finally here, because both men were amazing cooks and they'd already been told helping Patty was their number one priority.

The compound sat on sixty acres and well hidden from the main road by rolling hills and well placed rows of trees. The acreage was bordered with a slow moving cliff-lined creek along the back property line, that creek eventually fed into Lake Travis near Austin. They had one of the few open water level access points to the creek for miles in either direction and they hadn't hesitated to take advantage of it by building a large covered dock for entertaining. To the left as you drove down the long white slate drive was a small lake with water so crystal clear that you could easily see to the bottom despite the fact it was nearly thirty feet deep. They'd installed a lighted fountain in the center which was controlled by computers in the security office. Setting up the fountain had been fun for two former Special Forces soldiers who had been trained to work in any type of water conditions. Despite the fact their friends hadn't understood why they'd been like kids with a new toy project, it really had been like Christmas morning when they'd gotten to "play in the water" as Patty had called it. Kent and Don had laughed when Patty visibly paled after Kyle had told her the only thing missing was a good explosion.

The horse barn had been converted into a fitness center, including a full size boxing ring, a gym that would rival most commercial facilities, and both men's and women's locker rooms. The entire property was surrounded by beautiful oak and pine trees, and there were now several paved and rock lined walking trails and outdoor scene areas that were monitored by state of the art audio and visual equipment. All of the cameras were motion and sound activated so anyone using those areas was as safe as someone inside the club itself.

They utilized the enormous main structure as the

home to The Masters of the Prairie Winds Club. The BDSM club included a bar and dance area as well as several demonstration and stage areas. They'd added numerous themed rooms that could be easily opened up for the viewing pleasure of others if the participants happened to be exhibitionists. The basement had been transformed into a dungeon that looked like something the early Texas settlers would have assumed an old European castle would look like. He and Kent had enjoyed working with a designer to incorporate elements of both old west and Middle Ages traditions. All the basement walls and floors had been rough faced and the electrical wiring for the wall sconce lighting and monitoring equipment had been tap drilled so it was hidden from view. The entire dungeon was almost spooky in its realism. It was easy to forget where you were until you started looking around at the padded black leather equipment and the implement wall, which held over a hundred different devices. Most were for various types of impact play but there were other treasures hidden there as well.

Kyle and Kent shared the top floor's spacious apartment. Kent had turned the space into something that looked like it belonged in some fucking magazine in Kyle's opinion and of course that meant their mom had ooed and awed until Kyle and both of their dads had been rolling their eyes. Both Dean and Dell West had finally conceded that it was beautiful, but had steadfastly insisted it was also stuffy. Kyle spent most of his time in the media room or sleeping, so in the end the décor hadn't really mattered to him at all.

Kent had agreed to let Kyle design the rooftop garden and outdoor kitchen. And Kyle had made sure the area's casual ambiance made it a great place to relax and entertain. He'd chosen a hot tub that would easily seat ten people and the small outdoor kitchen area was perfect for their needs. The "patio" as it had quickly become known also had a hidden entrance to their personal playroom.

The playroom had been Kyle's favorite personal project and it really was something to behold. God, he was proud of that room. He'd intentionally made it as modern and sleek as possible because he hadn't seen any reason to create another dungeon when they had one just three floors below. Their personal play area had dark oak flooring and with its corner location meant there were two walls of windows and he'd lined the other two walls with mirrors. The closets, bathroom, and shower area were hidden behind mirrored doors and the equipment in the room was all stainless steel and black leather. Exposed polished steel beams lined the ceiling and chains on ball-bearing rollers could be positioned at almost any location throughout the room.

They'd spent almost a year remodeling and adding on to the main building, and then getting everything set up before opening just a few months ago. He and Kent had agreed that they wouldn't spare any expense, and the finished product was something they were both extremely proud of. Thanks to large trust funds from both sets of grandparents and their fathers' extremely sound investment strategies, money wasn't a concern for either of the West brothers. But being independently wealthy had never meant their parents hadn't pushed them to be the best they could be no matter what challenge they'd been facing. Both of their dads had believed in hard work and had passed that mindset on to both he and Kent. Both he and his brother had a tremendous amount of love and respect for all three of their parents and their parents' polyamorous relationship had never seemed odd in Kyle or Kent's opinions. As a matter of fact, he and Kent had decided when they were just kids that they wanted to share a wife as well.

Muttering to himself about the fact the storm seemed to be intensifying rather than abating, Kyle was momentarily blinded by another brilliant flash of lightning and it took him a few seconds to process the fact there had been someone standing in the middle of the highway. *Holy fuck.* Slamming on the brakes was his first instinct but he quickly backed off them when he felt the back of his truck begin to fishtail and he certainly didn't want his ass end swinging around and hitting a pedestrian. Thanking God above he hadn't been going fast because his reduced speed had meant he'd been able to miss the lunatic standing in the middle of the road by the slimmest of margins. Why someone would stand in the middle of a water-filled roadway in an electrical storm waving their arms was something Kyle just couldn't imagine. He slowly managed to maneuver to the side of the road and it took him a couple seconds to calm down his racing heart.

Kyle could almost feel the adrenaline pumping through his system as he grabbed a rain slicker from the back of his truck and pulled it on. It wasn't like it was going to make any difference with the rain coming sideways, but he felt better knowing he'd made the effort. Jumping down out of his truck, he turned around to face a very wet and extremely pissed off angel.

TOBI STROBEL WAS livid...completely over the top pissed. From the moment she'd burst into her boss's office at Austin Gardens and Homes and met Lilly West, her entire world had seemed to tip on its axis. Tobi had been on a tear about the interview she'd been trying to schedule with Prairie Winds "cad" owners, Kyle and Kent West. And she hadn't even bothered to knock before she'd blown into the small room like a Cat 5 hurricane. When the beautiful dark haired beauty had introduced herself as the "cads" mother, Tobi had wanted to melt into the floor. But Lilly West had been the epitome of grace and only laughed as she'd agreed that her sons were a handful for sure, even though she claimed to be withholding judgment on the "cad" determination. Tobi had felt drawn to Lilly in a way she hadn't really been able to explain, and the only reason she could come up with was because she'd lost her own mother when she'd been so young. The excuse sounded weak even in her own mind, but it was the only reason she could come up with…at least it was the only one she was willing to accept. Lilly had assured Tobi that her assessment of Kyle and Kent avoiding interviews was dead on and had promised to help her secure an appointment the following day. Before Lilly had left the small magazine's office, she'd given Tobi a long hug and then kissed her on the forehead saying, "They are going to be thrilled to finally find you."

Later that night Tobi had laid awake wondering at the woman's strange words, but her musings had been cut short by a text message from Kent West giving her directions to Prairie Winds and asking her to arrive at precisely seven the next evening. Tobi hadn't minded the fact she'd be giving up her Friday evening because she never really went out anyway. It wasn't like she had any disposable funds for entertainment, and quite frankly, her small apartment wasn't in a neighborhood that was safe to be out and about in after dark. What she hadn't planned on was the fact she'd be facing a storm so fierce she'd been forced to pull over to the edge of the road because she hadn't been able to see where she was going.

Thank God she'd left her seat belt fastened because she had no sooner put her small car in park than a large truck had barreled past and barely clipped her back bumper, sending her ancient Toyota nose down into a deep ditch. The ditch was rapidly filling with water, so Tobi grabbed her things, wrapped them in a couple of plastic bags she found under her seat and climbed back up to the roadside. Amazingly, not one single person had stopped despite the fact she'd been standing right at the road's edge.

The next time she'd seen lights headed her way, she'd moved to the center of the road and had begun waving her arms wildly over her head. Just as the enormous black pickup had gotten close, a bolt of lightning hit in the field to her right and the flash had illuminated the startled expression of a man Tobi could only describe as movie star handsome. She'd only gotten a glimpse of his dark intensity before she'd found herself jumping to the side to keep from becoming his newly mounted hood ornament. By the time he'd managed to screech to a stop, she was hopping mad and stalking toward the large black pickup as fast as her short legs would carry her. She was only five foot two, but as she liked to remind those around her, what she lacked in size, she made up for in attitude.

Tobi had almost reached his truck by the time he finally stepped out, "You almost ran over me. Holy smokes Batman you could have killed me with that monstermobile of yours. Damn, a drowned rat. My whole life is spiraling out of control faster than a Kardashian marriage I tell ya. Shit, shit, double shit. My car is probably floating toward the lake and my stuff is in trash bags. *Trash bags!* That's a whole new level of the wrong side of the tracks, even for me. I'm so wet I'm pretty sure I won't be dry for a month of Sundays, hell's fire I'll probably mold. And you are freaking huge and probably some serial killer on the top of some most wanted list. I'll end up on the evening news and my brother will never even know what happened to me because he refuses to watch the damned news. My crazy ass neighbors will pick apart my apartment before the broadcast is even over and I'll be a footnote on some unsolved mysteries show a few years from now. And I still don't know what Lilly West meant by finding me. Damnation this sucks big green donkey dicks I'm telling ya for sure." When she finally came up for air and realized the tall hunk in front of her was simply staring at her with his mouth in a grim line, all she could manage to do was blush. He had to be at least a foot taller than she was and his dark hair was barely visible under the Stetson he was wearing. His eyes were a deep chocolate brown that was quickly turning even darker. She realized she was staring at him just as he spoke.

"How do you know my mother?" Mr. Tall, Dark and Intimidating demanded.

Did he just say mother? That's it...that is the final straw. I'm officially certifiable and straitjacket ready. "Mother? Lilly West is your mother?" Looking up at the sky, she asked, "You're kidding me, right, God? First, you put their mom in my boss's office just as I have a meltdown about the infamous kink masters not returning my calls. And then of all the people on this planet, you let me almost get run over by one of the men I've been trying to schedule a meeting with for weeks? Is this some kind of a joke?" Just as the words left her mouth the world around them exploded in light and a crash of thunder that was so immediate she was sure the bolt must have hit right beside them. *Holy shit!*

Reminder to self…do not challenge the Big Guy.

"Get in the truck, *now*." His words had been more growled than spoken and ordinarily she'd be giving him a piece of her mind for thinking he could give her orders, but right now she was more afraid of becoming a crispy critter in the middle of the highway than she was of Lilly West's son. Tobi briefly wondered whether he was Kyle or Kent as she scrambled into the big black beast when he opened the door and motioned her inside, but judging by his clipped tone she was guessing Kyle.

She'd done her homework on the owners of Prairie Winds because she'd been hoping to interview them since she first heard about the BDSM club they were building just a few minutes from her home. Sure, she worked for a magazine that spotlighted all things bright and beautiful in the Austin area, but in truth, her interest in the club was much more personal. Banishing those thoughts for the moment, she turned and plopped her soggy ass in the passenger seat and turned to see him staring at her as if he'd never seen a woman before. *What the hell?*

Chapter Two

K YLE WEST HAD been speechless after he'd stepped from the door of his truck and almost been steamrolled by a tiny wisp of a woman who had reminded him of sunshine for some odd reason even though she looked more like a spitting mad wet kitten. Hell, she was seven kinds of pissed and ranting about a variety of things that hadn't made a lick of sense and he hadn't put too much effort into trying to sort through it until he'd heard his mother's name. He knew his brother was meeting with some reporter from Austin Gardens and Homes this evening, but the guy was supposed to have been at the club an hour ago. The beauty he'd been face-to-face with was not how he'd pictured someone named Tobi. Her long blonde hair was plastered to the sides of her face and even wet it was the color of sun-ripened wheat on a hot Texas summer day and he'd found himself wondering what it would look like dry. Would it be white blonde? Was it straight or wavy? Would it feel like silk as it covered his thighs while his cock slid over those plump lips?

He just stood in the middle of the highway in the pounding rain and let her vent until they had both almost been hit by lightning. Kyle had literally felt the air around them sizzle from the electrical charge so he'd quickly ordered her into his truck. When he'd opened the door and motioned her inside he hadn't expected her to comply so quickly and he damned well hadn't expected her to crawl all the way across the truck's bench seat. That move had displayed her luscious ass in vivid cock hardening detail thanks to the soaked thin cotton skirt she was wearing. The lightweight fabric was molded to her like a second skin outlining every sweet spankable curve. He immediately flashed to her bent over the spanking bench in their private playroom. They would tie her to the bench with silk scarves because she was too delicate for metal or thick leather cuffs. Then they would stand back to admire their handiwork before proceeding. Her ass would be a lovely shade of hot pink from the paddling she'd get for that smart mouth of hers. He wondered if she knew that she was a natural submissive. She might be full of piss and vinegar, but her instant response to his command to get in the truck had been telling indeed.

Climbing in, he turned to her and asked, "How far back are your things?"

"I...I don't know for sure. Maybe a quarter of a mile." He could see that she was starting down the slope toward an adrenaline crash and he wanted to get her to the club before that happened, so he quickly turned and headed back the way he'd come. When he'd seen her small hand move to the door handle as the bags came into view he'd told her to stay in the truck and he'd get them. "One has my laptop. It's really old, but it's all I have so please be careful with it."

"Will do." He'd tried not laugh at her because she looked so sweetly sincere, but he was fairly sure the computer was probably already beyond repair. The thin plastic sacks she'd wrapped everything in would have done very little to protect the sensitive electronics of a laptop. The lost look on her heart-shaped face caused him to stop and put his palm along her jawline and stroke his thumb over her cheek. There was something about her that made him want to shield her from anything that might cause her pain or unhappiness, and that certainly wasn't his usual reaction to an untrained submissive. "What's your name, kitten?"

"Tobi. Um…Tobi Strobel." Her voice was airy and he wanted to shout for joy at the way she unconsciously tilted her face and leaned into his touch. *Oh baby girl, you are a sub to the bone.*

"Well, it's nice to meet you, Tobi. I'm Kyle West. I believe my brother, Kent, was expecting you quite some time ago." Nodding toward her car in the water-filled ditch, he went on, "It's pretty easy to see why you missed that appointment and I promise to keep him from punishing you for being late, okay?" He didn't give her time to respond to his comment about punishment even though he'd clearly seen her pupils dilate when he'd mentioned it, instead he forged on. "Now, I'm going to get your things while you wait here." As he walked away from his truck he thought back on how her beautiful green eyes had widened in alarm a split second before they'd dilated with lust at his comment about Kent punishing her. It had taken a herculean effort on his part to not pull her onto his lap and crash his mouth over hers. He wanted to feel her lips opening at his demand and then he'd explore every corner of her mouth with his tongue before exploring the rest of her in the same way.

After he'd placed her small bags on the floor in his backseat, he climbed behind the steering wheel once again and headed to Prairie Winds. She didn't say anything and he'd noted that she had started shaking. After he'd turned off the main highway, he'd pulled to a stop before peeling off his rain slicker and wrapping it around her small shoulders. When she'd looked up at him, he realized her eyes weren't just green, they were a brilliant shade of green that bordered on neon. He just stared at her for long seconds before speaking, "We'll be at the club in a couple of minutes and then we'll get you dried off and you'll feel better—I promise."

She'd just nodded before whispering, "Thank you. I don't know what's wrong with me. I'm not usually this pathetic. But I feel like I'm sliding down a steep slope and there is nothing at the bottom to catch me."

He leaned to her and kissed the tip of her nose, "I'll catch you, kitten. Now sit back and try to relax. We're almost there." Before he started the truck, he grabbed his phone. Grateful when he saw he once again had reception, he quickly typed a text to his brother letting him know that he had Tobi and asked Kent to meet them in the garage—alone. He knew Kent would wonder why he would ask him to meet them, particularly when he specified he didn't want him bringing any of the staff with him. But Kyle knew his brother would figure it out soon enough.

KENT WEST WAS pleased to see a text from Kyle because he'd been worried about his brother traveling in the storm. Hell, he was already wondering what the hell had happened to that Tobi guy his mom had made him promise to talk to. All of their communication had been via email, but the guy had seemed solid enough that Kent hadn't expected him to blow off an interview he'd been badgering them to schedule for several months. He'd just gotten to the large garage they'd built behind the club when the door to Kyle's bay started to slowly ascend.

As soon as the truck was parked, Kent pushed off from the concrete column he'd been leaning against and approached the truck and wondered why the guy was waiting as Kyle walked around to the passenger side. Kyle was completely soaked, he'd shed his suit jacket and his white dress shirt was so wet it was almost transparent. Kent noticed the passenger's door still hadn't opened and for just a second Kent wondered if the reporter had been hurt. But Kyle's shit-eating grin was in direct contrast to that concern so he'd let it go. Kyle gave an almost imperceptible jerk of his head telling Kent to follow him.

When Kyle opened the passenger's side door Kent was completely stunned when he looked at the most breathtakingly beautiful woman he'd ever laid eyes on. Kyle had taken her small hand in his and helped her out of the tall truck. Kent unconsciously stepped forward and tried to hold back his smile at her confused expression. Even people who knew they were twins were usually shocked the first time they met he and Kyle in person because they really did look like the same person. Very few people could consistently tell them apart. As far as Kent knew, their maternal grandmother was the only person who had *never* confused them.

"Tobi, this is my brother Kent. Kent, meet Tobi Strobel, the reporter mom talked to you about." Kent looked up at Kyle and blinked in surprise. "Yeah, I'm right there with ya. Might want to have a chat with mom about the idiosyncrasies of information sharing." Kyle's soft chuckle had let Kent know he wasn't really annoyed with their mom, but he'd likely point out her error by omission the next time they spoke.

Kent wasn't used to being speechless and it had taken

him a few seconds to recover his infamous charm. He took in Tobi's appearance and that seemed to bring him back to the moment. She had started to shiver, so without saying a word Kent leaned down and scooped her up in his arms, then started for the door leading to the back elevator that would take them directly up to their apartment. He heard Kyle chuckle again behind him as he said, "I'll grab her things and meet you upstairs. Kitten, let Kent get you into a warm shower and I'll find something warm and dry for you to wear."

Kent looked down into the started face of the woman in his arms and smiled. "Sweetness, you are shivering and soaking wet. My brother and I would be remiss in our duties as the owners of a BDSM club if we didn't take care of you. Besides, neither one of us wants to explain to our mother how the reporter she seems to have taken a shine to caught pneumonia because we let her interview us while she was miserable in wet clothing." He leaned forward and kissed the end of her nose as he stepped into the small elevator. After pressing in the code for their apartment, he leaned back against the wall.

"You can set me down, you know. I *can* walk and I'm getting you all wet." Her voice was soft and light, making him wonder what she would sound like as she begged for release. Her eyes were hooded, telling him that she was either sexually sated or skating close to an adrenaline crash. And since he knew his brother wouldn't have fucked her in the truck, he was putting his money on option number two. He only hoped he got her undressed and showered before she bottomed out.

He heard her soft gasp as they passed through the apartment and he was looking forward to showing her around, but first she needed to be warmed up and dry.

When he entered the master suite's bathroom he started the shower so the water would warm up before he set her on her feet. He saw her eyes rake over his shirt, which was now plastered against his chest. The look of appreciation that passed over her expression made all those hours spent in the gym seem like time well invested. He'd stepped back a step, crossed his arms over his chest, and watched her study him. He smiled when her gaze reached his erection and her eyes widened. He'd been rock hard since the moment Kyle had helped her down from the truck, and from the look in her eyes, she hadn't missed his cock pressing relentlessly against the zipper holding it captive. When her eyes had slowly tracked back up to his and she realized he'd been watching as she checked him out, she blushed a lovely shade of crimson. He decided it was time to get her into the shower. "Strip."

Her eyes went wide and when she started to step back from him, he said, "Don't you dare." She instantly froze and he watched as her breathing became faster and he could see the pulse at the base of her neck pounding rapidly. When she didn't move he took a small step toward her. "Sweetness, I gave you an instruction and I expect you to follow it. I want you out of those wet clothes right now."

"But...you..." If he'd thought she was blushing before, well she was positively glowing now.

"Yes, I'm here and here I'll stay. This is the only time I'm going to give you a break on this so listen carefully. You already know that my brother and I are Dominants, correct?" When she nodded he continued, "And that we own the kink club you have been trying to get into for months under the guise of interviewing the owners, correct?" This time her nod was a bit slower. *Aha, I see the sweet little sub had figured out where this is headed.* He gave her a smile that let her know he was intentionally painting her into a corner. "It stands to reason that my brother and I have seen our fair share of naked women, correct? And in truth you are interested in more than the architecture of the club, have I gotten everything about right?"

This time she didn't even bother to nod, she just dropped her gaze and whispered, "Yes, Sir." At first he was sure he'd heard her correctly, but when he looked up at the door to see Kyle leaning against the frame with his arms crossed over his chest grinning from ear to ear, he knew he had indeed heard her correctly.

"Good girl, kitten. Now do as you've been told before you earn your first punishment before you even get your interview." Kent watched as Tobi's fingers slowly moved the small buttons at the front of her blouse. Her hands were trembling and he wasn't sure if it was from the cold or excitement, but it was easy to see that she wasn't going to get the shirt undone without help. Kyle stepped closer, "Here, let me help you. Your fingers are shaking. Are you still cold, kitten?"

When she shook her head quickly from side to side Kent stepped around behind her and then leaned forward to nip the lobe of her ear, "Answer with words, sweetness. Always with words. Be completely honest and don't hold back or edit your answers—ever. Do you understand?"

Kent knew he was pushing her, but he and Kyle had always believed that it was best to begin as you intended to go, so there was no reason to sugarcoat anything with her. "Yes, Sir." By the time she'd finished her answer they'd gotten her out of everything but her bra and panties. The woman was wearing lime green and neon pink underwear under that conservative outer layer and Kent wasn't sure but he might pass out when the last of the blood that had been feeding his brain started racing south.

Kyle looked at her and whistled softly in appreciation. "Damn, girl. You are fucking gorgeous. And as much as I love that color combination against your beautiful ivory skin, the bra and panties have to go." This time they didn't help her, but neither of them let their gazes move from her as they quickly stripped out of their own clothes.

"Oh…my stars…are you getting in there with me?" They had moved her to the open door of their shower and Kent knew she'd already forgotten her question by the way she was staring open-mouthed at one of his favorite features of the master suite. The shower area was ten feet long and almost a full eight feet wide. They'd installed several different types of showerheads and two different handheld units that had attachments, but he didn't think she was quite ready for those games tonight. He saw her hesitate to step all the way in when she noticed the floor to ceiling windows. "I…can people see us?" She might not think she wanted to be seen, but he'd be willing to bet his half of the club that she would eventually come to love it.

Kyle stepped over to the small control panel and the glass frosted instantly. "I think that might be fun, kitten, but we'll save that for another day. Now, let's get you clean, shall we?"

"You're going to wash me? Oh, no that just won't do. I'll do it. That is just too…well, it's too much." Kent landed a stinging swat to her ass and heard her gasp in surprise. "What the fuck was that for?"

This time he gave her two swats and made them just a bit harsher. Kyle leaned close and Kent watched as her nipples tightened even more as his brother's chest hair abraded them. "Careful, kitten, this doubling of swats could add up really quickly." Kent hid his smile when she nodded in quick jerks of her head but didn't say anything. *Smart girl, she learns quickly. Goddamn she is so gorgeous I can barely keep from pushing her against the glass and sinking into her sweet pussy.*

Kent started shampooing her hair and smiled at the sweet sounds of contentment she made as he massaged her scalp. "I think she likes that, brother, we'll have to keep that in mind for later. Kitten, when you are dealing with a couple of former Navy SEALS, water sports are a given. But right now, we need to get you finished up and out of here before you drop." Kyle had already taken his own quick shower and Kent did the same while Kyle put conditioner in Tobi's long hair. As soon as they'd wrapped her in a towel from the warmer, she started making all those cock teasing moans and groans again and Kent wondered how he was going to get through the interview now that he knew how beautifully she responded to their dominance. Of course, they didn't have to make any effort to get her back to Austin tonight and from the little bit Kyle had said, it was obvious her car wasn't going anywhere. Suddenly this evening was looking much more interesting.

Chapter Three

Tobi wasn't sure exactly how she'd gone from being spitting mad about her car being wrecked and then being nearly run over by Kyle West to naked in the shower between him and his brother. The two of them were hotter-than-hot sexual Dominants and she wondered briefly what it would be like to have their undivided attention focused on her. Talk about being run over by a freight train…mercy, these two might ask questions and she knew they listened to the answers but in the end, they would do what they wanted to do. *I wonder if anyone has ever said no to them.*

Feeling Kyle's hands massaging her scalp as he shampooed her hair had to be one of the most sensuous experiences of her life, and that was when she had suddenly realized that she was no longer cold. Oh no, not cold at all. As a matter of fact, she was downright hot in certain places and then they basically shut everything down and she was left wondering what she'd done wrong.

Remembering how disastrous her last foray into the mysterious realm of male-female relationships had been sent a shiver of regret and apprehension racing up her spine. Good God Gertie, every time she even thought about Chris Feldman, she felt an overwhelming urge to take a scalding shower. Why she had even agreed to go out with him was something she should probably go into therapy to explore. Not only did they work together, a dating situation she had always avoided like the plague, but she hadn't even been remotely attracted to him physically. He was a pompous ass at work and even worse on their one and only date. Sighing to herself, she knew the truth and she didn't like herself very much when she thought about how shallow she had been.

When Chris had dangled the Snowball Gala tickets in front of her like a carrot she'd caved and agreed to go with him. She had always dreamed of attending Austin's glitzy charity event and envied her friends that had been invited from time to time. But the entire evening had been one cluster after another. Chris had shown up to get her in a limo, which he'd gloated about and she knew he'd been sure his extravagance would impress her…it hadn't. And then he had wanted to have sex with her as soon as they'd pulled away from the curb. The thought of sex with him disgusted her and the idea of doing it as they drove through the streets of the city made her stomach threaten to revolt. Every time he'd touched her, she had found herself having to suppress a shiver of disgust. His breath had smelled of whiskey and cigarettes, and smoking had always been a deal breaker for her with dates.

By the time they pulled up to the Civic Center, she had been forced to re-do her hair because he'd continually tried to run his fingers through her long blonde curls. While she had been trying to put herself back to some semblance of order she'd been mortified to look over and see him stroking his very small cock up and down with frantic strokes of his beefy hands. When she'd asked him what the hell he thought he was doing, he'd told her that if she wasn't going to "take care" of him, he'd just have to take care of it himself. By the time she'd gotten into the ball, she'd been so upset that she hadn't enjoyed the evening at all. Feigning a headache, she'd called a cab and left early.

She refused to go out with him again each time he'd called her after that night. These past few weeks he'd started to get more aggressive in his pursuit of her and he had even been making off-hand remarks about her upcoming performance review, so now she was also worried about how the whole disaster was going to affect her at work. His calls had gotten more frequent and his language increasingly graphic and foul, and in the back of Tobi's mind she knew she should probably file a complaint at work, but she hated rocking the boat.

Shaking off that train of thought she decided that part of keeping her job would depend on how well this interview went, so she needed to refocus her attention on the task at hand. Her personal interest in the West brothers' lifestyle had to be tabled if she was going to concentrate on what she needed to do…the only problem was she was finding the two of them to be nearly irresistible.

From what she'd seen of their home, it was spectacular and she was anxious to get a closer look. Tobi found herself wondering if they would let her take a few pictures for the article, so many people objected to pictures of their homes being publicized now because of the obvious security implications. And while she understood their concerns, it sure did make her job a lot more difficult. She'd wait until they showed her around to decide what to ask for. She was going to have to fight her attraction to Kyle and Kent West and write a kick ass article if she had any prayer of keeping her job.

The magazine where she had finally found an entry-level position was cutting staff to the bare bones because readership had fallen off. With so much free information available on-line, people were reluctant to spend their dwindling disposable income looking at the luxury others lived in. Her reporting position at the magazine wasn't the best job, hell it wasn't even in her real area of interest, but it was the only thing she'd been able to find. Who knew a design and marketing degree was going to be so useless in the real world? *Damn, if I lose this job because of that asshole and have to move back in with my brother, I'm gonna go postal.*

Feeling like she was being watched brought her out of her thoughts and she looked up to see Kyle standing in front of her with his arms crossed over his muscled chest watching her intently. She felt her face heat and once again silently cursed her fair complexion. When he didn't say anything for several seconds she started to fidget under his gaze. "Kitten, I've asked you the same question three times and you didn't hear me or were ignoring me, I'm not sure which."

Uh oh, question? Damn it, I'm going to fuck this up if I don't yank my head out of my ass. "Um, could you repeat the question, please?" Almost before she'd finished speaking she felt two sharp swats on her bare ass. *Bare? What the heck happened to the towel I had wrapped around me? Jesus, Joseph, and Mary, maybe I should move back in with my brother and his family, I need a damned keeper.*

"Watch your language, sweetness. You are much too smart and attractive to talk like a gutter snipe." Kent's voice came over her shoulder startling her. Damn, she hadn't even heard him walk up behind her and she was usually wary of anyone standing behind her. The only apartment she'd been able to afford was in a neighborhood where being aware was a survival skill. *Shit, I said that aloud?*

Kyle put a finger under her chin and raised her face to

his and she found herself lost in his dark eyes. They were the most delicious shade of chocolate brown and she wanted to fall into them and never come out. Both men oozed sex appeal and authority, and she found herself wondering what they were like as Doms. They probably already had a gaggle of subs following their every order, and she had no desire to become a notch on their bedposts. And even though she was more than a little curious about their lifestyle, she wasn't sure she would ever be a good submissive because the thought of being humiliated for someone else's entertainment didn't do a thing for her. And as her brother would gladly tell anyone, she was pretty lousy at taking orders without asking a dozen or more questions.

This time when she came back to the moment Kyle was chuckling, "Kitten, I don't know whether to paddle you until you can't sit comfortably for a week, fix us both something to eat, or start addressing all those questions and comments I don't think you realize you've been speaking out loud—again."

"Out loud? Again? Oh crap on a cracker. I hate that, boy oh boy, you'd think I'd learn. But no, not this girl…I just keep on fu..um, fumbling things up with the same ole stupid behavior." She glanced over her shoulder to make sure Kent wasn't going to smack her again and saw him smiling and shaking his head.

"Good save, sweetness, but next time you'll get a swat for intent. Now, let's get you and my brother fed so we can chat a bit."

She suddenly noticed they were both wearing faded Levi's that looked like they'd been molded to their delicious bodies. When they turned and Kyle grabbed her hand to lead her from the room, she tried to pull her hand back but he just tightened his hold on her. "Wait. I can't eat like this...it's, well, it just isn't decent or sanitary or well...right. And what if someone else shows up? That elevator opens right into your home and somebody would see me, and I'm supposed to be working." They hadn't even acknowledged that she was speaking and suddenly she wasn't all that thrilled about being ignored. "Hey, are you guys listening to me? Jumping jack rabbits, this is really not going well at all. I have to do this interview and I have to, well, I mean I want to do a really great job."

Her words brought both men to an immediate stop and they stood together in front of her. "Kitten, we'll be talking to you more about the asshole that has become a problem for you at work. Congratulations by the way for not having sex with him. Obviously he hasn't figured out the meaning of the word 'no', but I have a feeling he'll figure it out soon enough." Tobi wasn't sure exactly what Kyle had meant by that, but he didn't look like he was in the mood to explain, so she kept that question to herself.

"Sweetness, as for your worry about someone seeing you naked in our kitchen, there are a few things you need to think about. Number one, do you believe we would ever hurt you or endanger you in any way?"

Kent's question surprised her and she was even more surprised to find that she knew without a doubt neither one would physically harm her. "No, I feel safe with you. I don't really know why, but it's still true."

Kent nodded, "Thank you. Your trust is important to us both, I assure you. Now, number two, that elevator is coded and *only* three people—my brother, the head of our security detail, and I know the code. So there is no chance we'll be entertaining surprise guests because Micah never comes up unannounced. And we might as well get this last issue out of the way right now. We'd planned to discuss it, among other things while we enjoyed our food, but if you are going to worry about things, let's get it done now. While we both are Doms and we enjoy a rather wide variety of BDSM activities, we aren't sadists. We don't play blood games or even allow them at our club. We also dislike anything that involves pins or needles of any kind. Piercings should be done by trained professionals and neither my brother nor I have any interest in becoming trained so you'll be safe on that point as well. Now, as for humiliation play, we don't particularly like it for ourselves, but you will see it happen in the club because there are some Doms and subs who enjoy it. Since it isn't physically dangerous we don't interfere. We have punished subs in ways they might have considered humiliating, but I assure you they ended up enjoying themselves immensely. We have never had a sub complain about the way we treated them, so you need to strike that from your worry list as well."

"Kitten, we promise to take very good care of you, but first let's get something to eat. I didn't get any dinner this evening and I doubt you did either. We'd like to talk to you and we like seeing your lovely body, but how about a compromise? I'll get you a shirt to wear, but you won't be allowed to button it or sit on it." *Sit on it? What an odd thing to say.*

She was pretty sure she'd heard a grunt from Kent at Kyle's offer and she didn't want to risk them snatching back the olive branch they'd extended so she quickly agreed. Kent pulled her the rest of the way to the kitchen while Kyle went back down the hall. By the time Kent had gotten her a bottle of water from the refrigerator Kyle had slipped a soft cotton dress shirt over her shoulders. He picked her up and sat her on one of the bar stools so she was facing the kitchen before pulling her knees apart and showing her how he wanted her to hook her ankles around the legs of the stool. And true to his word, he hadn't left the fabric under her bare ass and the cool leather had caused her to gasp. The thought of her bare girly bits against the seat made her pussy wet and wasn't that just great? *I'll probably leave a big ole wet spot and that's just gonna suck. Could I possibly embarrass myself more?*

Before he'd left her side he'd run his fingers lightly through her soaked pussy lips and smiled at her. "I don't think we mentioned it in the shower, but we were both pleased to see that your pussy is nicely shaved, kitten. Being able to see each and every response is a serious turn on for us both. Watching your pussy's lovely lips swell as it prepares for us and seeing your honey coating the soft folds is sexy as hell." She felt her whole body shudder in response and knew he'd felt her pussy moisten even more. When he withdrew his fingers she'd almost fallen off the stool watching him lick them clean before moving around her and into the kitchen.

While they worked together reheating the dinner their housekeeper had left for them, they'd kept her entertained with tales of their exploits as kids. She'd enjoyed hearing about all the trouble they'd gotten into and had found it easy to see the mischief making boys they had been. They had asked her about her job, but not specifically about the trouble she was having with Chris Feldman. She had always been uneasy sharing such personal information, but she had known those questions were coming. They had listened intently as she told them her worries about the staff cutbacks the magazine had been making and how perilous she felt her employment situation was. They had quizzed her about her degree and experience, and she'd felt they'd been asking for a specific reason, but she hadn't been brave enough to ask. It would be too much to hope for that they knew of a job somewhere, and rather than face disappointment or rejection, she just kept her questions to herself.

They'd eaten their meal at the small kitchen bar and she'd found herself relaxing more than she would have thought possible considering the day she'd had and the fact that she was sitting there eating with her legs spread wide and the shirt Kyle had given her gapping open in the front. The one time she'd tried to pull the edges together Kent had slapped her hands and opened it even further, admonishing her to leave it alone or she'd lose it and find herself over his knee as well. His words had made her pussy clench and moisture roll out in response to the picture that flashed through her mind. She wondered what on earth had happened that her body and brain seemed to be on totally different pages all of the sudden.

Chapter Four

K YLE DIDN'T REMEMBER the last time he'd enjoyed a dinner with a woman as much as the one he and Kent had just shared with Tobi. She was bright and had a great sense of humor. She'd asked thoughtful questions and had been open in her answers to their questions even when he'd known she had often been uncomfortable doing so. Granted they hadn't gotten around to the really hard questions yet, but they'd established enough of a baseline with her that at the very least it should be easy to spot any attempt she might make to evade the information they needed before they'd go any further with her. No doubt she'd seen their conversation as casual and free flowing, but as she'd eventually learn that was rarely the case when dealing with sexual Dominants. They had deliberately led the conversation and asked questions they knew would be easy for her to answer as well as a few that had caused her to pause briefly. By doing so, they'd learned her tells—those little signs of discomfort with a question or with what she was being asked to reveal.

After they'd finished eating, they'd moved to the media room. Kyle had started the stereo and fireplace and they had settled in to talk. Kent positioned her on the square coffee table in front of the sofa and reminded her to keep her legs spread apart. Then he'd positioned her hands flat on the table behind her, forcing her to lean back just a bit.

Moving her long hair over her shoulders, he'd watched as her eyes went from brilliant green to a dark moss color as they darkened with desire. Kent pushed the shirt off her shoulders and smiled when her pretty pink nipples had tightened even further. "Very pretty, sweetness. I am pleased that you didn't move your hands."

"Kitten, during your little mental meandering earlier you mentioned an interest in BDSM." He heard her small intake of breath and watched as her blush started directly over her heart and spread quickly upward. "Don't be embarrassed. Acknowledging your needs is important to your physical and mental health. People who continually live their lives in ways that are not meeting their needs end up prime candidates for heart disease, ulcers, and a host of other stress related problems." He waited a few minutes for his words to sink in and take root. She'd know he was right as soon as she used her mind instead of her fear to evaluate the information he had just given her.

"Now, we're going to ask you some questions and we want your complete honesty. As a matter of fact, we're always going to expect you to be completely honest with not only us, but with yourself as well. If you don't know the answer, say so and we'll move on until you do. Do you understand?"

"Yes." When he merely arched his brow at her, she quickly amended her answer, "Yes, Sir. I understand." Since she had an interest in Dominance and submission he was sure she had probably done at least some research. Her quick correction proved to be an accurate assumption.

"Very good, kitten. Thank you for that. Now, have you ever played before?"

"Played, Sir? Can you tell me what that means, please?"

Her question was an answer, but he'd explain it anyway, and consider it the first of many lessons. "Play is the word used to refer to BDSM encounters and/or interactions that are usually driven by protocol and are almost always solely directed by the Dom. But that doesn't mean the sub is powerless—in fact the opposite is actually true. Now, your question will serve as your answer to that question so let's move on."

Kent leaned forward and placed his hand on her knee and Kyle watched the muscles in her leg tighten and quiver beneath her satin smooth skin. She hadn't tried to pull away, but her body had certainly responded to his touch. "Sweetness, have you talked to anyone in the lifestyle about your interest? Or perhaps tried to get a previous sexual partner to experiment with you?" Kyle knew that Kent had nailed the second question, because Tobi's eyes had immediately dropped. She'd tried to mask the embarrassment, but he hadn't missed it and he was sure Kent hadn't either. It was a sad fact that many people felt like they were forced to hide their needs because they feared society's judgment. Since they'd begun the process of vetting club members several months ago they had heard a lot of versions of the story, but all of them had been basically the same. "I tried to get my partner to spank me to liven things up, but he said there was something wrong with me and I should get professional help so I never asked again." Oh, the genders and the requests had varied, but the abject humiliation of the rejection had been a recurring theme.

"Let me remind you about our earlier admonishment about being honest. And remember, sweetness, lying by omission, or editing is still lying." Kyle had been certain that Tobi's thoughts were scrambling for a way to *present* the information that would have been slanted at the very least and probably closer to downright misleading, Kent's warning seemed to have been enough to cut through her efforts.

Kyle bit back a smile as Tobi took a deep breath—damn but she was adorable when she was trying so hard to fight back her discomfort and be brave. "I mentioned it once to a boyfriend in college but he got pretty weird about it, so I dropped the subject. But that didn't keep him from telling all his frat brothers all the juicy details. Other than that all I know is from the books I read." She'd looked both of them in the eyes while she'd answered and Kyle had seen nothing but honesty even though it had been edged with something else, but he wasn't quite sure what it had been. Whatever the emotion had been, it was so fleeting he almost wondered if he'd imagined it.

"Thank you for your honesty, kitten. I know that was hard for you to answer, but we really do need to know exactly how familiar you are with the lifestyle. We'd like to take you downstairs later and walk through the club, but we wouldn't do that if it was going to frighten or upset you. You're apt to see any number of scenes being played out in the main room. We've seen inexperienced and ill-prepared people become very traumatized in the clubs we've visited over the years and that isn't at all what we want for you." He let his fingers trace slow circles on the inside of her thigh as she took in what he had said. "Now, how many men have you had sex with?"

Tobi's eyes became absolutely huge and the flush that rushed over her face was so bright he was surprised she hadn't moved her hands to fan herself. He'd seen this same reaction from subs for years and as a Dom had always found it remarkable. Men seemed to pride themselves on the number of women they'd fucked, but women were usually much more discreet in disclosing their level of experience. Usually Kyle viewed this question as little more than a normal part of a pre-scene negotiation, but this time it felt much more personal. If he hadn't been looking right at her and seen her mouth move ever so slightly, Kyle wasn't sure he would have heard her whispered, "Two." *Two? Holy shit, are the men in this woman's social circle blind?*

When he leaned further forward and brushed back the soft mass of white blond curls, his heart clenched at the sight of her unshed tears. "Kitten, tell me what about that answer put this sad look on your face."

To her credit her gaze never left his as she blinked several times trying to send the tears back into hiding. "Well, I know you are both really experienced. And I know that you probably have women chasing after you all the time." She took a deep breath and squared her shoulders as if she was getting ready to deliver something of monumental importance. "And I just can't see any reason you'd want to spend time with a chunky, inexperienced, likely soon-to-be-unemployed, born-again virgin."

Honest to God, Kyle had made what he'd considered a valiant attempt to hold back his laughter at the absurdity of her statement, but he'd failed miserably. His bark of laughter hadn't been without consequences because the tears she'd tried to banish began streaming down her pink cheeks with unchecked enthusiasm. The minute he realized that he'd hurt her feelings he pulled her onto his lap and positioned her so she was facing Kent. "Kitten, I'm sorry I laughed. I want you to know that I wasn't laughing at you in the way you think I was. First of all the born-again-virgin remark was just plain funny, as I'm sure you well know. But the other two things we're going to address right now. First, I don't really know anything about the employment situation, but losing the job you have now might not be the tragedy you believe it would be. And we'll talk about that more later on. Now, it's your reference to yourself as being chunky that my brother and I are both going to take issue with."

Kent pulled her tiny feet into his lap and immediately turned them out so her legs were opened to his view once again. "Sweetness, take it from two Doms who have seen their fair share of naked subs, both male and female, over the years—your assessment of your body is inaccurate. Personally, I've never been attracted to women who are rail-thin stick figures and I'm sure Kyle is going to tell you the same thing. I don't know who put that idea in your head, but I assure you we are going to help you silence that little internal voice that is plaguing you with self-doubt." If Kyle hadn't known his brother almost as well as he knew himself, he might had thought that was all Kent was going to say on the subject, but Kyle knew better so he just waited. *Wait for it...wait for it...yep, here is comes.* Kyle fought his urge to smile when Kent opened his mouth to continue, "And sweetness, this is the *only time* you will get away with making a disparaging remark about yourself. The next time you say something like that, you'll be over one of our knees with your bare little ass glowing a nice bright pink before you know what hit you. So I'd suggest you be very careful where and when you make that mistake again."

Kyle felt her entire body shiver ever so slightly at the thought of being spanked just a split second before the sweet smell of her arousal hit his nose. "Kitten, our club has very strict rules about things that have to happen before you can play in any of the club areas. Since we don't have your medical form on file and you haven't been screened for membership, we won't be able to play there tonight. But that doesn't mean my brother and I don't want you, nor does it mean that we will keep our hands off you while we are downstairs. We hope after you tour the club, you'll stay with us this weekend so we can all three explore what seems to be a mutual attraction."

Kyle let the words settle like dust in the room that had been stirred by her earlier uncertainty. He knew he was putting himself and Kent out on the very end of a limb in a strong breeze, but he also knew that was where the sweetest fruit was always found.

Chapter Five

Kent hadn't even realized he was holding his breath awaiting Tobi's answer until she finally nodded and simply said, "Yes. Yes, I'd like to stay. I have to know if I can do this." Sweet words to any Dom's ears because it meant she wanted to find out if her rational mind could accept what the sexual woman inside her craved.

Kyle turned to him and suggested, "You know, brother, since Tobi has been so honest and open with us, maybe we could give her just a small preview of coming attractions—say, a bit of a *prelude* if you will. What do you think?" Kent thought it was a fan-fucking-tastic idea that only had one major flaw–it wasn't going to do anything to ease his throbbing erection. *It's going to be a long damned night.*

He grinned at Tobi and watched as her eyes darkened and her breathing became quicker. The need was practically pulsing from her. "I think that is a wonderful idea." He and Kyle had shared women practically from their very first sexual encounter so they easily fell into perfect synch with each other. Kyle's mouth crashed over Tobi's and Kent slid his hand up the inside of her thigh and slipped his fingers up and back down through the soaking folds of her labia watching the lips swell and darken as they became engorged with blood. Seeing her body prepare itself for the pleasure it was on the fast track to chase, drove his own desire even higher.

Kyle had moved a hand so he was pinching each of her nipples alternately and Kent was thrilled to see her arching into that little bit of pain. He knew her body was already blurring the line between the pain and pleasure, and it was wondrous to watch. What many submissives didn't understand in the beginning was their body's inability to make the distinction between the two sensations when they were linked together. By adding the sharp pinching to the pleasure he was creating with his kiss, Kyle was confusing Tobi's senses and teaching her body a new way to respond to pain. And when you added in Kent's fingers circling her clit with random passes over the top of the little bundle of nerves, her body was completely centered on the pleasure.

"Sweetness, you do not come until we give you permission to do so. Do you understand?" Kyle pulled back from the kiss and waited for her to answer, but Kent wasn't too sure he hadn't waited too long to give the instruction because he could already feel the rippling of her pussy walls around the tips of his fingers. Hell, he'd just barely begun pushing his fingers inside her soaking channel.

"Kitten, did you hear Master Kent's instruction?"

"I…I don't know if I can hold…it. Oh, please…" Kent smiled because it was obvious she wanted to comply, but her body wasn't willing to wait. Truthfully, he had been so caught up in his relief she had agreed to spend the weekend with them that he'd missed that small window of time when he should have given her the instruction to delay her orgasm. If they punished her for something she truly couldn't control at this point, it would erode the small amount of trust they'd already built and would tarnish the release she was closing in on quickly.

In one smooth move Kent slid off the sofa, widened her legs and licked her quickly before blowing a puff of air over her pulsing pussy. "Come for us, sweetness. Show us your pleasure." Kent wasn't sure he'd ever seen a sub respond as quickly to his order to come as Tobi had. She'd already been arching before he'd finished speaking and the strength of her pussy clamping down on the fingers he'd pushed back into her heat was almost painful and he found himself fighting his cock's demands for relief just from watching her. Christ, he hadn't lost control of his own release since he'd been a teenager and here he was clamoring for control like an inexperienced youngster.

"Kitten, that was just about the most beautiful thing I've ever seen. And from the look on my brother's face, I'm sure I am speaking for him as well when I say you just upped the stakes for tonight exponentially. Now, I'm going to take you back and settle you in for a nap. I want you to rest a bit before we go downstairs, okay?"

Good call, brother, we'll each have a chance to take a nice long—very cold—shower and maybe find some relief.

As soon as Kyle headed down the hall with Tobi cradled in his arms, Kent flipped open his phone and called downstairs to ask their receptionist to send up something appropriate for their guest to wear tonight. After giving Regi fairly detailed instructions on what he wanted to see Tobi wearing, Kent started toward the hall that led to their bedrooms. He met Kyle who nodded toward the kitchen. Once they'd both grabbed a beer, they stood in the kitchen leaning against the counter—both of them lost in their own thoughts. He finally broke the silence, "I've asked Regi to send up something for Tobi to wear tonight." Kyle's smile told him that he understood Kent's unspoken message.

Regina Turner had been one of the first people they'd

hired for the club. She was barely five feet tall and he seriously doubted that she'd weigh ninety pounds soaking wet. She had an elfin quality that made her beautiful face look almost ethereal until her mischievous grin surfaced and then she had always reminded him of Jax McDonald's ornery younger sister. Regi might look like she belonged on a college campus, but she was wise beyond her years, organized, loyal, honest, and completely fearless. She was a submissive but there weren't many Doms strong enough to handle her so she didn't get to play as much as she probably wanted to. One of their goals was to find the perfect Dom for Regi, and as her self-appointed protectors, they planned to be very particular.

Even though the three of them had shared beer and pizza while watching football more than once, there had never been any sexual spark between the trio. Regi trusted them to screen Doms for her, but they all three knew they didn't personally have the right chemistry to play together so they'd never crossed that line. But the woman had killer taste in club wear and Kent could hardly wait to see what she sent up for Tobi.

The original design of the club had allowed space for a few venders to display and sell their wares so members would be able to keep abreast of the newest trends in all things kinky. It had worked out so well, they had recently begun discussing adding on in order to accommodate the rapidly expanding demand for more offerings.

"Jesus, I shudder to think what she'll send up. Hell, we might sooner get her down there stark naked than in something Regi picks out." Kyle's harsh words were negated by his chuckle and the shaking of his head. But his expression sobered and then he looked at Kent with all sincerity, "Do not fuck this up, Kent. This woman is special. There is something about her that calls to me, and the fact mom's involved is significant."

"Agree on all counts. Now, let's bring up tonight's scene schedule and decide what we're going to let her see. I want a variety, but nothing too severe." Kent knew Tobi would be totally unprepared for some of the things that were regular events on a weekend so they would have to watch her carefully. "I also asked Regi to send up a pair of red cuffs and a pretty choker. I don't want there to be any question about the fact she is not available for play." The red cuffs would be a signal to every Dom in the club that Tobi wasn't available and the chain necklace would just reinforce the message that she was already taken.

Kent had never liked the wide dog collars that some Doms favored because he had yet to see a woman that looked good wearing one and the humiliation associated with them wasn't a message they wanted their sub to feel. A woman's submission was a precious gift and he couldn't see a dog collar as a very appropriate way to show someone how cherished they were. He and Kyle had always loved the idea of their sub wearing a piece of jewelry that they all knew signified how important she was and that she belonged to them. Kent was the more design conscious of the two of them and he was already letting designs begin to take shape in his mind. A collar for Tobi would have to be dainty and something she could wear every day. He and Kyle would want it to be something she would be proud of and consider a gift rather than an anchor.

Kyle pushed away from the counter and tossed his empty bottle in the recycling bin, "I'm hitting the shower before checking the schedule. I'll use the shower in the master suite, I don't want Tobi to wake up and feel alone in a strange place. I'm also sending a large bouquet of flowers to mom." Kent laughed because he didn't need to ask why. They were both very close to all three of their parents, but they both loved their mom and respected her opinion. He finished off his own beer just as he received a text from Regi, so he sent the elevator down. When she said she'd loaded everything he called the car back up and waited to see what the little she-devil had put together.

Chapter Six

Tobi stretched and thought for sure she had fallen asleep on the softest cotton covered cloud in heaven. She hadn't even opened her eyes yet, preferring instead to just enjoy the feeling of the sheets skimming over her bare skin. *Bare? As in naked? Holy shit Sherlock, why am I...oh my God, what have I done?* Tobi was frantically searching her mind for some sort of rational explanation as to why she had allowed herself to get in this predicament, but nothing in her current arsenal of excuses was even coming close to covering the colossal mistake she'd made.

Sitting up clutching the sheet to her bare breasts that were still wonderfully sensitive from Kyle's earlier attention, she looked around the room in a frantic search for her discarded clothing. She leaned over to peer at the floor despite the fact she knew Kyle and Kent had actually stripped her in the bathroom. She hadn't heard the bathroom door open...actually she hadn't even considered where either of the West men might be until she heard Kyle's voice behind her. "Now there's a beautiful view. Damn, kitten, your ass is fucking perfect." When she jerked around, plopping her ass back on to the mattress, her quick movements sent a riot of blonde waves in all directions. Someday she was really going to have to get a handle on her unruly hair, but that wasn't going to happen today so she let the thought slide right back out of her mind.

"Oh, um…hi, I was just looking for my clothes. Have you seen them?" Kyle just stood over her watching her intently as he was studying everything about her for so long she was beginning to wonder if he was even going to respond. She was starting to question what she should do when he cocked his head to one side and smiled.

"Second thoughts, kitten? Do you always wake up with your thoughts all scattered about or is this an orgasm induced condition?" She didn't see anything but sincerity in his face, but there was definitely amusement dancing in the depths of his dark eyes. He was so good looking that she couldn't help but look at the contours of his face and wonder how God had managed to make two perfect looking men. And then she wondered what He was thinking by dangling them in front of her like a prize she could never really win.

"Well, I….damn it to Denmark, no matter how I answer those questions I'm gonna be in trouble so maybe I should just plead the fifth and call it a day." She hadn't meant to be flip and she had learned a long time ago that it was a rare person who really appreciated her humor so she really should have given her response more thought. She quickly dropped her gaze to her lap and watched her fingers pinching and twisting the sheet as if her hand belonged to someone else.

She hadn't expected the chuckle she heard from him and when she slowly raised her eyes to him, she so was surprised to see not one but two intimidating men standing over her with towels casually wrapped around lean hips. When the little black dots clouding her view started dancing, she realized she was holding her breath but couldn't seem to let it go. "Darlin', I do believe you better take a breath." She heard Kent's voice, but her attention was on the matching six-packs directly in front of her. *"Now!"* The sharp tone of Kent's command had her gasping in the oxygen her brain was desperately seeking and thankfully the black dots of death as she'd always called them dissipated into mist. Ever since she'd been a kid she would catch herself holding her breath when she was particularly nervous and it was a habit she'd always hated. She and her friend and neighbor had laughed when they had discovered they shared the bad habit. Gracie was one of the best friends Tobi had ever had and they were so much alike it was almost scary sometimes.

Tobi took a couple of gulping breaths of air and when her head finally cleared enough to speak she looked up into the now stern looks on Kyle and Kent's faces. "Sorry, I guess I sort of panicked there for a minute."

"Kitten, if that was panic in your eyes, I'm worried about what your real sexual hunger might look like. Don't lie to us—ever. Now, I'm going to give you one chance to amend that statement so don't blow it." She was pretty sure he'd used that expression on purpose and her face heated to near scorching at the image that flashed through her mind.

"Well, I really was panicking and it happens sometimes when I first wake up." Even though what she'd said was true, she didn't have any intention of explaining it. "And then I remembered where I was…and what I've done and I," she felt the first tear race down her cheek, "and I can't even imagine what you must think of me. Can you please tell me where my clothes are?"

Kyle sat down on one side of her and pulled her onto his lap. "Kitten, I don't know what you are thinking, but I can assure you that you haven't been asleep long enough for all the adrenaline to have moved out of your system."

She didn't know exactly what that meant and he must have noticed because his smile was filled with such compassion and understanding that she felt her heart clinch. "You are reacting in fear because of the hormones that are battling for supremacy in your system. And kitten, we're not going to let you make a decision based on fear." He pulled her close and kissed the tip of her nose before setting her on her feet. "Now, let's get you up. We'll let you primp a bit before we show you what our wild and wacky receptionist sent up for you to wear. By the way, you are going to love Regi, just try not to let her lead you into too much mischief, okay?"

Feeling much more settled, Tobi found herself looking over at Kent and wondering if Kyle's words applied to him as well. Kent's sexy smile helped settle her nerves and she turned to walk to the bathroom when his hand wrapped around her upper arm. His grip wasn't angry, but it was unyielding. "Sweetness, I saw the questions in your eyes and I want you to know that unless you are told otherwise, we will expect you to ask each of those questions respectfully. Don't assume you know the answers to what we are thinking. If you wonder, then ask." He didn't release her, but just continued to watch and wait.

Tobi barely resisted the urge to fidget and raised her eyes to his. "Well, I was just wondering if Kyle's words were...well, if he was speaking for you as well. I don't like feeling needy, but I really wondered, you know?" She had started out looking into his eyes but had let her gaze drift down because she didn't want to see the disappointment she was sure was there.

When he forced her face back up she saw his smile. "Now, that wasn't really all that painful, was it? And yes, Kyle also was speaking for me. Unless we correct the other one, you will always know that we're on the same page, got it?" The kiss he gave her made her knees weak and when he finally released her, she wasn't sure she was going to be able to walk unassisted into the bathroom. Before she turned from him he smiled, "Drop the sheet, sweetness. We want to see what is ours for the weekend." Even though she had been ready to leave just a few minutes ago, an odd sadness moved through her at the idea they only wanted her for two more days. But deciding this was likely the only chance she'd ever get to visit The Prairie Winds Club, she knew she had to suck it up and enjoy the time she had with them.

Letting the sheet slide softly down her body and puddle at the floor, Tobi stepped over it and started for the bathroom. She heard both men growl and she fought her own smile, because just knowing that she had been able to elicit that response from the two men behind her was immensely satisfying. They made her wet just by speaking to her and a little bit of turn-about was fair play after all.

"JESUS. SHE HAS absolutely no fucking clue how gorgeous she is. It's the damnedest thing I've ever seen and it's positively electrifying." Kent had meant every word he'd said after the door closed behind Tobi. Closing them out was something they would never allow her to do if she really was their submissive, but since she wasn't really theirs—yet, there wasn't much he could do about it. Turning back to his brother it wasn't difficult to see the hunger in his eyes as he continued staring after Tobi. "Come on, you need to see what Regi sent up."

He had been thrilled when he'd seen the dress their

friend had sent up for Tobi. The deep emerald color of the fabric had golden flecks in it that would set off her pale hair and green eyes as well as catch the lights. The halter dress was barely going to cover her generous breasts and it looked like the back was going to dip all the way to the top of her ass. And he loved placing his hand atop that particular erogenous zone, particularly when it was bare. The dress was also likely much shorter than what Tobi ordinarily wore so she would protest and that would give them the perfect excuse to use the small matching butt-plug Regi had included. *He made a mental note to send Regi a basket of all those imported chocolates she loved so much.* The dainty golden choker had small stones that would look perfect with the flowing dress along with the long dangling chain that would fall clear to the middle of Tobi's bare back. The gold was highly reflective and the piece was going to look spectacular against her perfect skin.

After he'd shown Kyle the bounty he'd laughed as his brother whispered, "Fuck, we aren't paying that woman nearly enough. Christ, this stuff is beyond perfect." Kent couldn't have agreed more.

"Let's get dressed so we can dress her. I have to tell you, I'm really looking forward to the hissy I know she is going to throw about how short this dress is. That plug is the perfect *funishment* for what we already know is coming. Hell, I'm not too sure that Regi isn't a closet dommé." They quickly parted and went to their own smaller bedrooms. When they had designed to penthouse apartment atop the club, they had agreed that the master suite would be reserved for a time when they found a woman that they wanted to share. It struck Kent as ironic that by unspoken agreement they'd settled Tobi in that suite rather than taking her to one of their bedrooms like they had with the other women they'd played with. Granted they had only invited two women into their personal space since they'd moved in, but he still hadn't missed the significance of their actions. Several minutes later they met back in the office and were checking the club's scene schedule when Tobi's soft knock sounded on the doorframe.

LOOKING UP TO see Tobi completely covered in the silk robe he'd left on the bed for her was the sexiest thing Kyle had ever seen. It didn't matter that she'd had to roll up the sleeves to find her hands and the damned thing hit her just above her ankles. She looked like a little girl wearing something her big brother had left unattended and still the picture was heart stopping. He held out his hand to her and was thrilled when she padded barefoot over to him and placed her small hand in his much larger one. "Kitten, I really like seeing you in my robe. And knowing that you are naked under it makes it even better."

Her nipples were already tight and displaying themselves beautifully through the silk, Kyle watched as Kent leaned forward and sucked one of the little beauties in without even baring it. He must have been biting down ever so softly because Tobi's soft sighs had morphed into a needy moan. When Kent leaned back he smiled up at Tobi's glazed over expression. "The robe does look lovely on her, but I prefer her without it. Hand it over, sweetness." Kyle fought a smile as she seemed to be having trouble bringing herself back to the moment and focusing on Kent's words. When Kent lifted an eyebrow in question she finally seemed to remember what he'd told her to do and slid the robe off her shoulders and handed it to him.

In the future her hesitance would earn her a punishment, but for now they were more interested in building her trust and compliance would be a natural by-product. As the robe had slid off her shoulders Kyle could see that she'd found the lotion they'd left out for her because her skin looked almost dewy and the scent of citrus and sage wafted over his senses making every nerve ending sit up and take notice of the beautiful woman standing naked in front of him. Leaning forward, he slid his hand up the inside of her thigh forcing her to move her legs apart. "The first thing we want to explain is the use of safe words. Since you've researched the lifestyle some, I'm assuming you know what that means, is that right?" When she nodded and answered affirmatively, he continued. "We'll use the club's stop light system. Green means you are good to go. Yellow means you want things to slow down or you have a question about what's happening. And if you say red everything stops. We'll discuss what went wrong, but we won't play again until we've all taken a break, rested, and talked it through. Now, we're going to show you two poses, kitten. There are several more, but these are all you'll need for tonight. You are going in as our guest tonight, but there are still some hard core members that won't like the fact we have allowed you inside if they don't think you are a sub at the very least."

He waited a couple of seconds until she'd had a chance to take in what he'd said before he continued. He'd learned years ago that when a sub's senses were being bombarded with new sensations and their emotions were running high it often took them longer than normal to fully process information. That realization had saved him and the subs he'd played with a lot of grief over the years.

While it was true they owned the club and as the owners they could easily override a member's demand for punishment if Tobi was to act inappropriately, that wouldn't serve any of them well in the end. Their plan for the club had always been not only that it would follow the cardinal rule of "Safe, Sane, and Consensual" at all times, but that everyone—even he and Kent—were subject to the "Rules of the House."

Some of their members weren't people they personally liked, but they'd met the club's criteria for membership and had made it through several levels of screening. Each new member was personally screened and investigated by Micah Drake. Micah caught a lot of guff about his looks, and Kyle had heard subs in the clubs refer to him as the Beefcake Dom. Standing well over six feet with shaggy blonde hair and crystal blue eyes, Micah was often mistaken for a southern California surfer even though he'd been born and raised in the Texas hill country. Micah had been the computer guru on their SEAL team so when he'd decided against re-upping, Kyle and Kent had talked him into moving back to Austin. They'd helped him open a private investigation firm and then promptly secured his services for Prairie Winds. If the prospective member passed Micah's scrutiny, their references were called and interviewed at length. Passing that level meant they spent at least an hour being questioned by both he and Kent. Micah had managed to send through the cream of the crop, so he and Kent had really had a pretty easy time of it when it had come to the personal interviews. The great thing about their system was they knew each of their members personally—that didn't mean they *liked* each member or necessarily that they respected them, but they did *know* each member on a first name basis. The familiarity had helped them know which members were sticklers for the smallest details of protocol and several of them were scheduled to be in attendance tonight.

Kyle pushed Tobi's legs further apart than he knew was comfortable for her and then showed her how to lace her fingers together at the small of her back. The position displayed her breasts perfectly. "Kitten, if one of us tells you to *present,* this is the position we'll expect you to assume immediately. We won't ask for this randomly so if we do, there is a compelling reason and you'll need to do it quickly and without question. I'm reminding you of this because there are several members of the club that will be watching you closely and we don't want to give them any reason to demand that either we take you in hand or that we allow them to mete out a punishment."

The change in her demeanor was almost immediate. She started shaking so violently at her core that Kyle actually placed his hands on her hips to keep her from falling. "Kitten, what's this about?" Her reaction was so out of proportion to what he'd said that he couldn't help but worry they were making a serious mistake by taking her downstairs. The frown on Kent's face told Kyle that he was also concerned about Tobi's reaction.

"I...please, I don't want anyone else besides you to touch me." She was looking back and forth between the two of them with a desperation that spoke to the sincerity of her fear. True fear was something every Dom watched for and gently explored, but always respected. And since Tobi wasn't really their sub or even a member of the club they would absolutely make sure no one touched her but the two of them.

Kent leaned forward and put his hands on each side of her face, "No one will touch you, Tobi. Well, I'm sure you'll get a hug from Regi and probably Tank, he's the bouncer at the front door, but they are both staff and friends of ours." This wasn't what Tobi had meant and they all knew it, but Kyle understood why Kent was mentioning it. Regi was always a force to be reckoned with and Tank's size alone was intimidating as hell. He wasn't particularly into the lifestyle, but he was protective as hell of the subs and damned good at helping up front. Tank had played professional football for the Cowboys, but two serious concussions in one season had forced him to decide if his sports career was worth the risk to his life. Tank had told them that when the doctors had explained the likely consequences of a third head trauma the decision had been easy.

Once Tobi seemed to have gotten her fear under control, they quickly taught her the kneeling pose. She was truly a natural with the positions and when they'd inquired about her flexibility she'd blushed. She explained she had been practicing yoga for years as a way to try to keep her weight down while staying toned and to control the stress in her life. Both of those were issues Kyle planned to address with her if their relationship worked out the way he and Kent were hoping it would, but he let the comments go by for now.

"Here's the dress we want you to wear this evening, kitten." He held up the dress and her eyes went impossibly wide with an expression of pure appreciation before it quickly changed to shock. Feigning confusion, he looked at her questionably, "What's the matter? Don't you like it?"

"Oh don't even try that hokey innocent nonsense with me, Kyle West. You know perfectly well what's wrong with it. Where is the *rest* of it?" Oh, she was playing into their hands beautifully and he had to fight the urge to rub his hands together like some dastardly villain in an old melodrama.

"Oh, sweetness, be very careful. You are skatin' on very thin ice here. This is actually a fairly conservative dress as club-wear goes so you might want to check the attitude before you earn yourself a punishment." Kent's words sounded stern, but his eyes were alight with the humor of the situation and Kyle knew his brother was battling to keep from laughing as well.

"But it's obscenely short and there's no back at all. Crapamolie, I'll be lucky if the crack of my ass doesn't show." Kyle watched her look around before she refocused her attention on the two of them. "Where's the panties? And shoes? You can't expect me to go without underwear or shoes."

"We do indeed expect exactly that." He'd already secured the choker around her slender neck and let his fingers follow the chain down her back, smiling at her shiver. "Now, let's slide this on and see how you look, shall we? Arms up." Kyle was actually surprised that she raised her arms over her head and he quickly pulled the dress down and positioned it so her pretty rose-colored nipples were covered before re-tying the halter behind her neck after Kent had lifted her hair out of the way. He and his brother stepped back and both twirled their fingers in the air, signaling her to turn in a circle. That was all it took for the last of the blood that had been in his brain to gallop south to join the party heating up in the other head. "Sweet baby Jesus. You look fucking amazing, kitten." Kyle knew his voice had gone from stern to reverent and he couldn't even manage to care because the woman standing in front of him was a walking wet dream.

Kent's voice sounded as strained as Kyle's had felt, "Stunning. Sweetness, you are absolutely stunning. Regi really deserves a raise for helping us with the clothing. That color looks amazing on you." Tobi's sweet cheeks flushed at their words and Kyle wondered if she had anyone in her life that ever said anything nice to her.

Kyle watched her look between them and then down at herself. "But it's really not decent. Not to mention it's probably a size *or two* too small. If I sneeze, my boobs are going to fall out unless you have some of that double stick tape. God forbid I should even try to bend over because strangers are going to see things they aren't supposed to see, if you know what I mean. I think it's a perfectly nice *blouse*, but you can't really expect me to go around flashing my bare ass to everyone can you?" And there it was. The perfect lead in. Damn if she hadn't just handed it to them on a silver platter.

Kent stepped back from her and crossed his arms over his chest. "You agreed to spend the weekend with us, Tobi, and to do as you were told, isn't that correct?"

"Umm, yeah, but…oh damn." Kyle had to cough to cover his snort of laughter because she'd figured it out quicker than either he or Kent would have dared hope.

Kyle reached into the small bag he'd set behind the desk and pulled out the plug and a new bottle of lube. Tobi's eyes went wide and she started to back up but froze in place when he raised a brow at her. "Kitten, you've earned this punishment. Because you have been uncooperative, you'll be wearing this pretty plug in your ass tonight. Since you were worried about people seeing your bare bottom, we'll just give them something else to look at." He snapped the lid on the bottle and started lubing the plug and his fingers. "Bend over the edge of the desk, kitten. Spread those legs nice and wide and arch your back so your sweet rear hole is where I can get to it easily."

Kyle thought his heart would stop when she complied so perfectly. "Well, brother, it seems maybe our sweet subbie likes this more than she wants us to know because her pretty pink pussy is practically dripping she is so wet." He emphasized his point by deliberately curving his fingers just enough to be sure they'd make a nice slurping noise as he worked them in and around her pussy. When he started rimming her ass with his finger smoothing the lube all around and massaging it gently into the tight ring of muscles around her puckered hole he heard her sharp intake of breath. "Have you ever been fucked in the ass, kitten?" He knew the words were crude, but he'd done it deliberately to see how she reacted to the tone and language, and he was rewarded with a breathy denial and fresh flood of moisture over his fingers. "Push back against my fingers, kitten. Good girl, like you would if you were going to try to push me out."

Kyle looked over at Kent and almost laughed out loud at his pained expression. When his brother finally looked up, Kyle gave him a quick signal with his other hand and Kent's smile told him that he was on board with the suggestion. "You know, brother, I'm not sure a butt plug is going to be enough of a lesson for our woman. She doesn't seem to be having to exactly *participate* in this punishment, if you know what I mean." Oh Kyle knew exactly what Kent meant and Tobi was going to have a crystal clear idea as well in a few seconds. Kyle leaned forward and slid his arm under her, moving them both back away from the desk just enough for Kent to position himself in front of her.

Chapter Seven

Kent pulled Tobi back so her face was just inches from where his cock was pressing against the zipper of his pants. He was going to be lucky if his dick didn't have a permanent zipper imprint. Kent had been so intent on watching the wide-eyed look she was giving his crotch that he hadn't even been able to speak yet and he was grateful for his brother's intervention.

"Kitten, open up his pants. Have you ever given a blowjob before?" Kent watched as Tobi tried to process Kyle's words at the same time her body was being bombarded by so many new sensations. Kyle hadn't stopped pressing his fingers slowly inside her ass and Kent smiled as he watched her slowly move her hands to the snap on his jeans and then work the zipper down. Since he went commando his throbbing cock had sprung free immediately and bobbed in front of her startled face.

"No. Well, I mean yes, I tried, but I don't think I did it right." She had answered the question, but her eyes had never left his cock. She seemed to be studying it as though she'd never had the opportunity to look at one close up.

Now that he wasn't worried about the zipper "tattoo", Kent was able to refocus his attention where it belonged. "Why don't you think you did it right, sweetness?" Kent would lay money he already knew what she was going to say. It was a safe bet some asshole had convinced her that his inability to perform was her fault, he'd heard the story too many times.

"Well…he didn't…you know."

Kyle leaned over, picked up the plug, and positioned it behind her and Kent could see his brother was trailing it back and forth over her puckered hole. "No, we don't know. Tell us."

Tobi swallowed hard before answering, "Well he didn't come." Kent had to work hard not to roll his eyes and saw Kyle's jaw flex in anger as well.

"And I supposed he let you think that was your fault?" Kent was threading his fingers through her silken hair and he knew the truth before she even answered because the humiliated look on her face said it all. When she slowly nodded, he had the sudden urge to find the man and horsewhip him.

Kyle leaned down and nipped at her shoulder, "Well, kitten, let's up the stakes a bit shall we? If you make Kent come before I make you come, I won't give you a spanking. But if you come first, you'll lay over my lap and get five swats before we go downstairs. Go."

Kent barely saw her move before his cock was enveloped in the most delicious moist heat he'd ever experienced. She sucked him deep immediately and swallowed around him sending electrical charges of pleasure racing up his spine. "Fuck me! If this is 'not good at it', God save me from her when she becomes experienced. Holy fucking God in heaven." Honestly Kent didn't see any way he was going to last for more than a minute—two tops. Her mouth was like heaven—with suction. Shit she was going to suck him dry in less than a minute at this rate. "Kyle, you'd better hurry or she is gonna win this thing by a country mile."

He'd only just managed to growl the words before Tobi sucked him in so deep he felt the end of his cock slide down into her throat. *Christ doesn't she have a gag-fucking-reflex?* The blood was pounding in his ears and then she hummed deep in her throat and the vibration sent him into orbit. He felt the hot seed jetting from the end of his cock almost before he realized he was flying into space. Brilliant colors flashed behind his eyelids as his eyes rolled to the back of their sockets. It was a damned good thing he was sitting down because there was no way his legs would have held him up. Hell, he wasn't sure they would hold him up an hour from now.

Kent was barely cognizant of the fact he had floated back to earth. Tobi had licked him clean and his happy member was laying contentedly on his leg. Watching as Kyle sent Tobi over by fucking her ass with the plug had him getting hard again, but he wasn't sure he'd survive round two right now.

Just as Kyle pushed the plug into place he'd had told her to come for him and her scream had been what every Dom lives for because it was instantaneous and rasping in its desperation. Kent smiled at his brother then moved his gaze to the sweet woman with her face in his lap, gasping for air. He stroked Tobi's hair back from her face, "I know I should go get a warm cloth for you, sweetness, but honest to God I don't know if my legs will work yet." He chuckled softly and added, "Stay still while Kyle cleans you up a bit."

It didn't take them long to get cleaned up and they'd even managed to get Tobi to drink most of a bottle of water before they headed downstairs. On the plus side, Tobi seemed much more at ease with the dress she was wearing, but on the negative side, Kent could still feel the muscles in his legs trembling. While they were in the elevator, he pulled her against his chest and kissed her. Pressing his tongue along the seam of her lips so she opened to him, he swept her mouth and relished the soft mewing sounds she made. "Sweetness, I don't know if I told you, hell I'm not sure I was capable of telling you—but that blowjob was way beyond *good*. It was fucking amazing. And I thank you." He pulled her closer and whispered in her ear, "And way to win the race too by the way." Kent laughed out loud and Tobi giggled at Kyle's grumbling curses behind them.

EVEN BEFORE THE elevator doors slid open, Tobi could hear the pounding of the music. She'd done her homework and had been expecting loud heavy metal music, and she was pleased to hear the familiar strains of a country western honky-tonk song. Kyle smiled at her, "Wasn't what you were expecting was it?"

She laughed and shook her head, "No, it wasn't. But this is better, I assure you. I love Kenny Chesney and his Caribbean beat totally rocks." She grinned up at him, "Will you dance with me later?"

Kent turned her so her back was to the room, "Yes, I will be more than happy to dance with you. Now, you need to remember to address us as Sir or Master while we are down here. I know it's going to sound odd to you at first, but you'll hear the other subs using those titles so you'll get the hang of it quickly. Until you are a regular club member you won't need to keep your eyes down, but I would still recommend that you be very careful about meeting the gaze of any Dom we are not specifically introducing you to."

Tobi nodded her head and then remembered and said, "Yes, Sir." Kent kissed her on the forehead and then turned her back to the room. They kept her between them as they made their way through the large room that included the bar and the large dance floor. He could see she was trying to take in everything but the place was so large and filled with so much activity that she was having trouble keeping up with them.

Kyle laughed at her and pulled at the hand he'd been holding. "Come along, kitten. We'll give you plenty of looky-loo time in a bit. First we need to check in with the staff and see how things are going. We're usually down here long before this so we're going to be playing catch-up for a bit."

THEY MADE THEIR way to the bar and were greeted by a man that surely had to be a giant. All Tobi could do was stare up at him. *He has to be the tallest person I've ever seen in my life. I'll bet he is seven feet tall. Wonder where on earth he buys clothes? Oh leapin' lizards in Laramie, I wonder how he gets in a car?*

The blonde man sitting next to where she was standing burst out laughing before turning to her. "You must be Tobi. I'm Micah Drake and the *giant* over there is Tank. He is usually at the front desk with Regi, but I'm guessing she's sent him for her caffeine fix." Tobi wasn't sure what to do, she hadn't intended to speak the words out loud. She immediately stepped back and came up against a hard chest. She heard Kyle's soft laughter as he wrapped his arms around her, settling them under her breasts so they were dangerously close to escaping the narrow confines of the halter dress she was *almost* wearing.

"Kitten, Micah is our security chief. He is also a private investigator in Austin and has an office there as well. And don't worry about your observations about Tank, I assure you he isn't offended, are you, Tank?"

"Oh hell no—it happens all the time. Nice to meet you, Tobi, and welcome to Prairie Winds. Hopefully I'll get to chat with you more later on. But right now I need to get this back to Regi before she goes bat-shit on somebody." Tobi found herself smiling back at him because he'd been so gracious about her faux pas and had gone out of his way to make her feel welcome. When he'd gone a few step, he turned and stepped back toward her, "You have any trouble with anybody, you give me a shout, you hear?" When she grinned at him and nodded eagerly, he smiled and walked away.

She'd looked up at Kyle and saw he was smiling and shaking his head. "I swear the man is pure magic with women. They all have that same deer-in-the-headlights stunned expression the first time they see him, but it only lasts until he speaks to them. After that, they all become his best friends. They show up at his house all the time with food and crap. It's fucking amazing, I tell you." He turned his gaze from the group standing around them to her specifically and said, "And before you even ask, no—he isn't gay or bi-sexual. He's straight and if somebody could market that *charm*, for lack of a better word, they'd be a billionaire by the end of the week." Tobi could only smile and nod in agreement, because he was absolutely right.

Looking around her, Tobi took in the room and wondered who had designed it because it was the most modern looking saloon she'd ever seen. Somehow the architect and designers had managed to utilize the western theme favored by so many Texans and incorporated modern concepts and materials with remarkable results. When she got up the courage to ask about pictures she was also going to ask about taking a few in this room...not wide angle shots, but focused views of certain elements like the wrought iron framed mirror hanging behind the bar. The frame was scrolled metal and from a distance it looked like black lace, which was no doubt exactly what it was supposed to look like since it was in a BDSM club. But it was the curved metal staircase that she couldn't take her eyes off of. The steps were at least three feet wide and the outside of the curve looked like a series of western scenes with a definite *kink* factor. The entire thing was painted so it looked aged and there were lights lining the inside so all the kinky scenes looked like simple illuminated silhouettes until you got close. The detail of the work was staggering and the craftsmanship made it a genuine work of art.

"Who did your metal work?" Tobi knew she wasn't really supposed to speak out while they were in the club but she was so totally enthralled with the entire place protocol hadn't been her first concern. When no one answered her right away she looked up at Kyle and saw the questions in his expression. "When I was in high school I took a welding class and I loved it. I had a teacher who appreciated the fact I'd taken the class because I was interested in learning how to weld rather than meeting guys, so he took a shine to me and helped me a lot. I even ended up taking the class again before I graduated. And then I helped out in a small fabrication shop for a while during college to earn extra money." She felt her face flush at the idea she'd shared something her brother had sworn was over-the-top tom-girl even for her and he'd thrown such a fit she had finally quit.

Kent stepped up behind her and whispered in her ear, "Sweetness, I can't tell you how thrilled I am that out of this entire room you picked two of my favorite features. Damn, you are fucking perfect." His soft chuckle in her ear sent a rush of moisture to her sex and she shuddered. "We worked with Clint Bollinger at E.G.A Fabrication in Sealy. The guy is a metalwork genius. I'm not sure anybody can dream up something he can't design and build. Look up. See the railing that looks like huge strands of barbed wire? He made that as well and wait until you see some of the headboards and canopies he's created for the private rooms upstairs, they are works of BDSM art. We'll introduce you to him if you like. His shop would be a great out-reach story for your magazine. He is a vet—a former Marine. Even his business name reflects that pride, it stands for Eagle, Globe, and Anchor, which are on the Marine Corps emblem."

She nodded up at him and grinned, "That would be great...well, if I still have a job in an issue or two." She'd tried to keep her smile in place even as her stomach knotted in worry. She was actually worried sick that she was going to be sleeping on her brother and sister-in-law's sofa again because she didn't even have a car to sleep in now.

Kent leaned down and spoke against her ear, "Stop worrying, sweetness, we aren't going to let you sleep on your brother's sofa. And we damned well wouldn't have let you sleep in your fucking car."

Damn, I really have to break that damned habit.

KENT KNEW TOBI hadn't meant to speak out loud, but

damn it was endearing and handy as hell, so he hoped she didn't ever break the habit. As he'd watched her take in the room, she hadn't tracked the people like most newbies. Often subs got in trouble for staring at Doms and their subs because they were either frightened by what they were seeing or totally intrigued and couldn't take their eyes off the action. But Tobi seemed interested in the details of room itself and that gave him a lot of satisfaction because he'd been heavily involved in the design of everything that had caught her attention.

Kent would readily concede there were far more interesting parts of the club, but there were still scantily clad male and female submissives in a variety of activities all around them. There was a sub laid over her Dom's lap getting swats just a few feet from them. The sound of flesh colliding with flesh would have gotten most subs' attention in the blink of an eye. Kent didn't know what the pretty sub had said that had gotten her up-ended so quickly, but her Dom almost had steam coming out of his ears. If Kent's memory served him well, the beautiful redhead was a prosecutor in Austin so it was hard to tell what a woman who made her living arguing might have said to elicit such a reaction.

Handing Tobi the bottle of water he had opened, he cautioned her, "Drink this, kitten. BDSM is hell on a sub's hydration level." He winked at her and laughed when she turned bright red. "Your blush is adorable and it makes you look perfectly fuckable. Now come along, we promised you a tour."

He watched as she turned back to Micah and stuck out her hand, "It was nice to meet you, Mr. Drake. I hope to see you again." Kent wasn't sure what surprised him more, her thoroughly "un-submissive" action or the stunned-into-silence look on Micah's face. Obviously Tobi's action was a longtime habit that was pure modern career woman in polite-mode and it warmed his heart to know she'd be getting a lot of paddlings if she became their sub—and that thought alone made him smile.

Micah finally regained his voice and just shook his head, "Tobi, darlin', you are gonna be a joy to watch." Then he looked between Kent and Kyle, "Enjoy her, I think you've finally found *her,* boys." Kent and Kyle both nodded in acknowledgment and led Tobi away.

"I wasn't supposed to do that was I?" Tobi's voice was quiet, but he'd still heard her question and the insecurity behind it.

"Kitten, you surprised him because he isn't accustomed to that behavior inside the club itself. And if you were already a club member that would have probably earned you a couple of bare-assed swats right then and there." Kyle grinned over her head at Kent because he knew his brother was thinking the same thing he was—Tobi was going to be a joy to train. Her openness and honesty would be both a gift and a curse at times, but she was completely genuine and Kent couldn't remember the last time he met a woman he liked as much.

They walked Tobi out to the reception area and introduced her to Regi before making their way around the club. Kent saw the hesitance in her eyes and smiled when he saw the recognition in Regi's eyes. "Wow, it's great to meet you, Tobi. I'm thrilled you are here, I can use some help keeping all the male staff around here in line, damn it's just too big of a job for one woman, I'll tell ya for sure. And Master Kent was right too, that color looks amazing on you." Kent watched as the stiffness in Tobi's shoulders seemed to relax as she warmed up to Regi. He honestly thought the two women could easily become good friends because they were actually fairly similar creatures, as his gramps used to say.

They stood back and simply watched Tobi and Regi's interaction for a few minutes, giving Tobi a chance to relax a bit more before they took her into the more *interesting* portions of the club. Kent noted that Tobi was unfailing polite even in the beginning when she was a bit more standoffish. But as the women got to know one another he could almost see her true personality emerging. He had already noticed that she'd obviously been raised in the south because she was gracious even when she seemed uneasy, but the thing that stood out the most was the fact she seemed to make the person she was talking to feel like they were the sole focus of her undivided attention. She and Regi had bonded in just a few minutes and Tank was standing to the side looking at Tobi as if she'd hung the moon and the stars.

Tank looked over at him and quietly said, "Makes me wish I'd been the one out driving in the storm. Damn, she is smart *and* beautiful. And you know what? I don't think she has any idea how gorgeous she is, and damned if that doesn't make her even more beautiful." Kent and Kyle both nodded because there just wasn't anything left to add to Tank's assessment.

Kent reached for her hand and pulled her back flush against his chest. Kyle smiled to himself as he watched a shiver move up her spine. Kyle wasn't sure what Kent had said against her ear but she had instantly gone bright crimson and he'd seen the pulse point at the base of her neck beating wildly after his brother's whispered comment.

Kyle grinned at her, "Kitten, I don't know what my brother said to you, but I surely do like your reaction to it.

Now, say goodbye to your new friends so we can go look around a bit." Both Tank and Regi pulled Tobi into quick hugs and reminded her that all she had to do was give either of them a shout if she needed anything.

As they started to leave, Regi caught their attention, "Oh, I nearly forgot to tell you. Some guy named Chris called here a while ago looking for Tobi. I tried to explain that I didn't know who he was taking about, but he was pretty insistent that I give her a message." She smiled at them with a devil's glint in her eyes before continuing, "Of course I didn't write down his words, because that would imply that I knew she was here, but I did note the number because he sounded kind of nutty. Anyway he was ranting about her losing her job if she doesn't call him tonight, so if you see her," Regi rolled her eyes dramatically and then giggled, "please let her know. Okay?"

Kyle reached over and ruffled her hair as if she really was the little sister they thought of her as being. "Well done, Reg. I'll take that number and return his call." Kyle saw Tobi's mouth come open but his glare registered and she slowly closed it and stayed silent.

"And Master Kyle, if you would be so kind as to explain to him that calling me a flaming bitch and incompetent c-word for doing my job isn't the best way to win my cooperation, I'd sure appreciate it." Regi's eyes had flashed with anger and Kyle had the sudden urge to send Micah and Tank into Austin to teach the asshole a lesson or two about how to speak to women.

Kyle was sure Regi knew full well the effect her words were going to have on all three men standing close but Kyle wasn't sure she had anticipated Tobi's reaction. "Excuse me? He said *what*? Oh, dear God of all things holy, what on earth was he thinking? Any man who thinks he can talk to a lady that way needs to be...oh never mind, that wouldn't be nice for me to say in mixed company. But honestly, I don't know what I should expect out a man who looks like the Mayor of Munchkinland in the *Wizard of Oz* and thinks it's acceptable to play with his wee-winkie in front of a woman on their first date." Tobi's whole body shuddered and then she froze as she realized what she'd said. "Well drown me." Kyle saw her shoulders sag and she looked up at him and his brother with such a bleak expression he wondered what had put that look in her beautiful green eyes.

She took a deep breath and turned to Regi. "Can you please call me a cab? I'll just run upstairs, gather my things, and clear out. And I'm really so sorry for all the trouble you all have gone to, but I think it's pretty obvious this isn't going to work out."

To Regi's credit she didn't move to make the call, she just stepped up to Tobi and pulled her to the side. Regi's hands went to her hips in that no nonsense stance each member of their staff had encountered at one point or another and the little imp leaned forward. "Let me tell you something, sister. That isn't the way we do business around here. We don't run and we don't hide. We back our friends and family, and we don't draw a line between the two either. So you can just put that self-sacrificing bullshit on the shelf. Suck it up and cope. Now, tell us how to deal with this asshat." By the time Regi had ended her little rant, her foot was tapping on the floor at close to ninety beats a minutes and she was almost vibrating with frustration.

Tobi blinked at Regi several times as if she was too shocked to speak before a huge grin spread over her pretty face. The sadness and defeat evaporated from her body language and she pulled Regi into a bone-crushing hug. "Oh you are just the best, you know that? My friend, Gracie, is the only other person who has ever done that. Nobody else has ever cared if I stayed or went. Thank you." Kyle saw tears in both women's eyes when they parted and he didn't know how he was ever going to repay Regi for the gift she'd just given Tobi, because having a friend that isn't afraid to call bullshit when it's needed and who has your back come what may was a gift that couldn't be replaced.

Chapter Eight

WALKING THROUGH THE club's largest lounge and scene area, Tobi felt like she'd stepped right into one of the her erotic romance novels she loved to read late at night. The sounds that assailed her senses were almost enough to make her come and the West brothers were barely touching her. The pulsing beat of the music provided the perfect background for the moans that accompanied the slapping of bare flesh against bare flesh. She'd already heard two women screaming and they had only walked about six feet into the room. Tobi knew her eyes were wide open and her mouth was probably gapping as well, but she didn't know what to do about any of that because she was really having to concentrate on putting one foot in front of the other…and breathing. Breathing had suddenly become something that wasn't automatic any more, nope she was actually having to make an effort to draw oxygen in.

There was just so much to take in and Tobi hated feeling like she was a peeping Tom and spying on people in their most private moments, but she couldn't make herself look away either. After thinking it over for all of thirty seconds, she decided that since they had chosen to perform out in the open, they must not mind being watched. Obviously, modesty wasn't the word of the day at Prairie Winds. *Yes indeed. That is my excuse and I'm going to cling to it until my last gasping breath.* But mercy, some of these people were just straight up having sex out in the open and Tobi had never actually considered how she'd feel about watching others in the midst of what she'd been raised to consider extremely private.

She hadn't even realized that she'd stopped walking until Kyle placed his hand against the small of her back and spoke against her ear, "Kitten, come along. We want to see what interests you. Don't worry about watching, but be respectful and don't speak out. If you have a question tap on our knees and we'll lean down so you can ask it quietly." *Lean down? What does that mean?* Obviously her confusion had been clearly written in her expression because he chuckled. "You'll see soon enough."

With gentle pressure against her back he led her toward a small raised platform where a larger woman was tied so she was facing a St. Andrew's cross. Tobi wondered why she was facing the cross and also the audience but then she noticed the large circle on the floor and knew the whole thing probably turned like a giant lazy-Susan. The woman looked like she was probably in her late forties and she certainly wasn't model thin but she looked entirely comfortable being nude in front of the gathering crowd. When both Kyle and Kent sat in leather wingback chairs she looked at them blankly for a few seconds before she noticed the large pillow on the floor between them. Kent's voice finally penetrated the fog that had taken over her brain, "Kneel, sweetness."

She remembered the pose they'd taught her earlier and nodded. "Yes, Sir." She slowly lowered herself to the pillow and positioned herself exactly as they had taught her. It wasn't particularly uncomfortable, but she sure was open to the view of the Dom on stage.

"That was beautiful, kitten. We're very proud of you. Now, let's watch Master Albert send his sweet wife, Chloe, over the moon, shall we?" Kyle's words had barely registered when the Dom they'd called Master Albert started rolling Chloe's nipples between his fingers. Suddenly he pulled clamps out of the pocket of his leather pants and attached the alligator clamps to the peaked tips of her bountiful breasts before tightening them until she squeaked.

"You can take more, my naughty girl. Don't you go wimping out on me already. You know why you're here and I'm gonna share it with everybody as they watch me put you through your paces." Tobi thought the man sounded mean and she was worried about Chloe until he turned toward the audience and his entire face lit up in a grin. "As some of you know, my Chloe is a judge in Austin. Well, it seems she was up for a big promotion and she failed to mention that fact to me *until* she was appointed to the position yesterday by our Governor." The man's obvious pride in his wife's accomplishment made her smile and even though she heard applause around the room, she kept her hands in their position.

Kyle leaned down and whispered in her ear, "Oh kitten, that was perfect. You didn't move and that is going to get you a nice reward later. And just so you know, Master Albert is none other than Albert Westfall, the owner of Westfall Oil." Tobi knew her eyes had probably gone wide but she wisely kept her lips sealed tight.

When the applause died down the man smiled again and Tobi noted that he was probably in his late fifties but it was obvious he took a lot of pride in keeping himself physically fit. "Thank you on Chloe's behalf, but I'm going to *torture* her a bit to remind her that these are the kinds of things she is supposed to share immediately with her Master, not months later." Tobi failed to fight her smile at how he was so obviously dramatically playing up her "offense" for the purpose of their scene. She froze when he glanced over at her smile and for just a second Tobi panicked, but when he winked at her, she felt her muscles relax.

Tobi watched as Master Albert moved to the side and rotated a small dial on the wall and the platform began a slow rotation. He'd stepped back over to Chloe and placed his hand on her shoulder while she was turning and Tobi could see him whispering to her the entire time. This time Kent was the one who leaned down to speak to her. "Master Albert knows that sometimes the movement of the stage is disorienting for subs because their senses are being bombarded by so many different stimuli that even the slow movement can cause dizziness. By touching her shoulder and speaking with her, he is able to distract her attention and prevent that. Remember, a Dom's most important task is always the safety of the sub who has entrusted herself to him."

They continued to watch as Master Albert used a flogger that looked like it was well broken in. The soft strips of leather left growing patches of color as he methodically moved it over Chloe's back and ass in perfectly timed movements. When he started down the insides of her legs Chloe's groans were finally becoming louder and even Tobi could tell the woman was getting close to orgasm.

"Don't you come yet, naughty girl, I'll tell you when you're allowed to let go. Your pleasure belongs to me, baby." Tobi could hear the strain in the man's voice and she didn't doubt that he was fighting his own release as well.

Tobi barely heard Chloe begging, "Please Master, it's too perfect. It's going to take me and I don't want to misbehave again. *Please* let me come." Her voice was so breathy that Tobi had barely heard the words laced in between her panting breaths. Suddenly Tobi felt her own release start to build. When she tried to focus on not jumping on the bandwagon barreling through the room, she realized she was holding her breath and starting to weave back and forth as those damned black dots made another appearance.

Tobi felt like she was going to pass out any second but then she felt the warmth and strength from Kyle's hand on her shoulder and his breath against her ear, "Breath, kitten. In and out nice and slow. We don't want to break Master Albert's concentration by taking you out of here if we don't have to. Your responsiveness is absolutely amazing and a total fucking turn on, just so you know." Tobi was grateful for his diversion, and after a couple of deep breaths, she felt much better. She was still worried about coming even though no one had touched her…she didn't even want to think about how embarrassing *that* would be.

Kent leaned forward as well and ran his fingers through her soaked folds several times. "Sweetness, you are fucking perfect. You are so wet, I'd say it's a given that we'll be introducing you to the joys of flogging." He must have felt her stiffen because he quickly added, "The strands start out as a tingle that lights up your skin and sensitizes you to even the softest touches and wafts of air. As the blood is drawn to the surface, the heat follows and is a delicious kind of pain that you crave as the finest pleasure. Master Albert used nipple clamps with small swinging weights so each breath his sub takes reminds her that she belongs to him…her pleasure is his to give when and if he decides to.

You, my sweet sub, have permission to come as soon as Chloe does." *Oh mercy, please Master Albert, please, please let her come.*

KENT COULD FEEL Tobi's sweet cream rolling over his fingers as she became more and more aroused by the scene. He and Kyle had both been happy to see Albert and Chloe on tonight's roster because not only was Chloe comfortable in her own skin, a lesson Tobi certainly needed to learn, but Albert was an easy going Dom who wouldn't care if they used his scene as a teachable moment for Tobi—as his earlier wink had proven. The Westfalls had been friends of his parents for many years and he and his brother had been thrilled when the couple applied for membership.

Smiling to himself, Kent remembered the conversation they'd had with their dads when they had decided to open a BDSM club. Even though it was common knowledge that their dads were Doms and their mom was their submissive, both of their dads had jokingly said they didn't believe they would *ever* be playing at Prairie Winds.

Dean and Dell West had inherited a mildly successful shipping and transportation business and turned it into a multi-billion dollar a year conglomerate. Even though the company was still privately held, their dads had recently mentioned they were considering going public. They knew appointing a Board of Directors and hiring a CEO was the only way they could take a step back from the crazy schedules they'd kept for the past thirty plus years. No one had told Lilly yet, but their dads had purchased a large ranch that adjoined the Prairie Winds property. Kent's understanding was they planned to tell her later this month at the surprise party they'd planned for her birthday. He also knew that both of their dads were so excited about the purchase he doubted they'd be able to wait that long. Besides, he'd never known anyone to be able to fly low enough to avoid his mom's radar for very long.

Kent knew his mom was going to jump at the chance to live near them once again, especially if she already thought Tobi was the one he and Kyle had been looking for. Laughing to himself, Kent was certain she was going to be working fulltime to make sure they convinced the little beauty kneeling between them to be theirs. And then Lilly West was going to become the chief engineer for the "I Want Grandchildren Now" railroad and she'd run over anyone standing on the track to get to her destination.

Kent watched as Chloe neared the point of no return and smiled as Albert dropped the flogger to the floor and stepped around the cross so he was facing is lovely sub. Albert's face pressed against his wife's ear and his fingers plunged into her dripping heat. When Kent saw her body stiffen, he grabbed a handful of Tobi's blonde waves, and tilted her face back and stared into her startled eyes. "Come" was all he managed to command before he sealed his lips over hers. Just as Chloe screamed with a release that seemed to go on forever, he caught Tobi's scream and felt her come all over his fingers as he fucked her with them. Her body clenched his fingers so tightly that he was sure she was going to send him over all too quickly once he finally had his cock inside her.

When he finally released her lips, she was gasping for air and the glazed look in her eyes was the look every Dom dreams of seeing on his sub's face. Kyle's voice sounded like sandpaper as he spoke along Tobi's other side. "Kitten, that was amazing. Watching you come on my brother's command was spectacular. Christ, this may be the shortest tour of a BDSM club in history."

After congratulating the Westfalls on an extraordinary scene, they moved on through the large room. They'd given Tobi another bottle of water and she'd downed most of it before smiling up at them. "I think you are right about dehydration being an issue, mercy. But I really could use a restroom break if you don't mind."

TOBI WALKED INTO the spacious ladies lounge and even though she didn't see anyone, she heard female voices. "Did you see the blond toad that Masters Kyle and Kent are escorting around the club? I wonder who is paying them to babysit their chubby sister?" The first woman's voice was brittle sounding and Tobi didn't hear any accent so she knew the woman wasn't a local.

"No clue, but she's a piece of work. At least they had the decency to put red cuffs on her so no Dom would play with her." This voice was pure southern bitch. Tobi had been dealing with women like this her entire life. Women who had been lucky enough to be born on the *right side* of the tracks and weren't about to let the "have nots" ever forget their place.

Tobi felt like her feet had suddenly become cemented to the floor. If she didn't move quickly they were going to find her standing there, and she didn't want to deal with that drama. But her dammed feet wouldn't move despite her mind's pleading insistence. The women had continued their catty remarks but it had faded to the background as Tobi concentrated on not crying and getting her feet to cooperate. When she felt soft hands on her shoulders she jerked her head up and saw the woman who had been getting a spanking earlier in the bar.

"Come on" was all the pretty redhead said to her as she guided her back out of the lounge. When she stopped in front of Kyle and Kent they both looked up and creases formed between their brows.

"Noelle? What is this about?" Kyle's voice was stern but Tobi knew it was with concern, not anger.

"There was a problem in the lounge. Take care of your girl here and I'll be right back. Oh and don't let anyone in until I come out, okay?" The woman's smile couldn't be described as anything but predatory and Tobi didn't even try to suppress her shiver as Noelle turned and stalked away.

Kyle turned his attention to Tobi and the look on her face must have told him how close she was to the edge. "Kitten? What happened in the lounge?"

Tobi opened her mouth to speak but before the words could come out the tears she'd been holding in slid down her cheeks. She would swear she heard both men growl but they were all quickly distracted by the sounds of raised voices coming from the lounge. The noise didn't last long and was followed by a few grunts and moans, and then nothing but eerie silence. The man that Tobi assumed was Noelle's Dom had joined them and Kent had quickly explained why they were all staring at the bathroom door. He started chuckling and shook his head before looking at Tobi, "Honey, are you okay?" When she nodded numbly he went on, "Well no offense sugar, but you look a little shell-shocked. I'm guessing somebody in there wasn't very nice to you, am I right?" *How did he know that?* "The only time Noelle goes off the deep end is when she is defending someone. How the hell she ever ended up as a prosecutor is a mystery a cluster of Mensa members wouldn't be able to unravel."

Just as he's finished speaking, Noelle walked out of the room and smiled sweetly at her Dom. "Hi, Master. Sorry I was delayed. Just had to help Masters Kyle and Kent out with some housekeeping." Looking over at Tobi, she stuck out her hand, "Hi, I'm Noelle Chambers. You're Tobi, right? It's nice to meet you. I wish it hadn't been under these circumstances, but I'm betting your Masters take care of um…what's left of the problem in short order. Welcome to Prairie Winds by the way." Noelle quickly explained to the men that she'd walked in right behind Tobi and had heard the remarks of the two women before hustling Tobi back outside.

Tobi reached out and shook Noelle's hand even though she wasn't sure she was supposed to and quietly muttered her thanks. Kyle introduced her to Noelle's Master, Neal Chambers, before the couple wandered away. Tobi had never felt more defeated than she did at this moment. The women's comments had brought each and every one of her insecurities right back to the surface. She just let her eyes drift to the floor wishing it would open up and swallow her whole. How had she ever thought she could fit in here? What in the name of creation had possessed her to imagine men as good looking and successful as Kyle and Kent West that they could possibly be interested in her?

The past few minutes had been a brutal reminder of why social classes have existed for centuries and don't appear to be fading anytime soon. Tobi hadn't even seen the two women involved, but she'd be willing to bet she knew exactly what they were about. When she heard the door in front of them open she looked up and had her worst suspicions confirmed. Both women were young, model beautiful, and perfectly built. Sighing, Tobi just looked back at the floor. Kyle had stepped up behind her and wrapped his arm around her protectively as he pulled her back against his chest.

Kent stepped in front of the women who both seemed to be walking gingerly. "Stop. You two find your Doms and meet us in the office in three minutes. Do not be late." His voice was razor sharp and when he glanced at his watch, they both scampered off like frightened rabbits. Kent turned back to her, "Sweetness, we should have explained that while it is true the red cuffs are a signal that you aren't available for play, we put them on you because you aren't a club member yet and quite frankly we didn't want any other Dom hitting on you. So our reasons were both business and selfishly personal." His sweet smile started melting some of the ice she'd suddenly found herself enclosed in.

Kyle turned her in his arms and leaned down to kiss a tear track from her cheek. "Kitten, those two have both tried more than once to get us to top them. We have steadfastly refused and have always tried to be polite in our refusals. But they obviously are not getting it. I can assure you they are going to understand completely in a few minutes. While we hash this out, we're going to have you sit with Tank and Regi. They'll be thrilled to spend time with you and if I had to guess, Noelle has already given them a heads up. That woman is one very bright cookie and she would have seen this pow-wow coming a mile away."

Kent's chuckle surprised her, "Hell, my guess is she is marshalling the troops and is planning a tar and feather surprise party for those two as we speak. We haven't known Noelle long, but it's easy to see that she is a firecracker. Sweetness, you'll be safe with Tank and Regi, and I promise we won't be long. But I don't want you exposed to the negativity this meeting is going to produce so we won't include you." The soft strokes of his thumbs over her cheeks were soothing and suddenly the events of the day seemed to be catching up with her, all she wanted to do was curl up in a ball and sleep until she managed to forget the harsh words she'd overheard.

It was obvious as soon as they entered the small reception area that Kent had been right. Regi and Tank had definitely already been given the scoop and they were wound tight. Regi sprang out of her chair the minute they walked in. "Shi…shih tzu puppies on a stack of sauerkraut Tobi…are you okay?" Tobi was so confused by what Regi had said that she just stared at her new friend who was practically vibrating with anger.

Kyle laughed, "Regi, I swear your saves from you cursing get more creative every time I hear one. But you better break that habit before we find a Dom for you or you're gonna be spending a lot of time over the spanking bench, darlin'."

"Yeah, yeah, yeah. I know, but the creativity is part of my charm. Now, Tobi. How are you? Boy those hags have been seven kinds of nasty to anybody they consider competition…so in a way maybe they were giving you a back-handed compliment."

"I'd like to use my hand on their back-something." Tank's comment must have surprised everybody because when he looked around and saw everyone staring at him he just grinned sheepishly and shrugged. "You all are contagious. Damn, my mama warned me this was gonna happen." His impish grin was such a contrast to his size that Tobi couldn't help the giggle that bubbled up from deep in her chest.

Walking over to him, Tobi pulled him down by the placket of his western shirt and kissed him sweetly on the cheek. "Thank you for that, Tank. I wouldn't have thought anyone could make me laugh right now and you did in under five seconds. You are amazing."

When she pulled back, his face was bright red and his murmured "you're welcome" was so quiet she almost didn't hear him.

"Well damn, now I don't know if it's safe to leave our lovely sub out here alone with Casanova or not." At Kyle's words, Tobi jerked her attention to him and was relieved to see he was grinning. She wasn't sure she was ever going to be able to be a good sub. She'd been on her own and struggled for so long to master all the social skills required for today's business world that she wasn't sure she wanted to "unlearn" those hard-earned habits either.

"Alone? Hey! What am I? Chopped liver?" Regi's indignant voice sounded from the side and Tobi couldn't help but laugh again. "Go on. We'll be fine. And the sooner you deal with those two, the sooner you can get Tobi back upstairs…she looks like she is about to crash." Regi was right, but Tobi wouldn't have made an issue of it.

Kent pulled her against his chest and whispered against her ear, "Sweetness, please let Regi take you to the employee's lounge. Or at least settle back in one of the chairs out here so you can lean back and rest a bit." She nodded and then stepped back as the two women and their escorts entered the small area. Tobi noticed the men looked mad as hell and one of the women looked contrite while the other clearly didn't think she'd done a thing wrong.

By the time Tobi had settled on the soft chair behind the reception desk she felt like she was running on fumes. She leaned her head back and decided to close her eyes for a few minutes. In the back of her mind she realized someone was lying a soft blanket over her and then she just let herself fall over the edge into the peaceful abyss of the fatigue she'd been fighting for too long.

Chapter Nine

KYLE DIDN'T REMEMBER a time he'd been as angry with a club member. One of the subs, a brunette named Mary, had acted remorseful, but only after they'd separated the women to interview them so it hadn't really earned her any points with either he or Kent. But the blonde had been a flaming bitch from the beginning. Kelly Mason would be walking out of Prairie Winds for the last time if Kyle had his way. Both Doms had quickly agreed to step away from the whole mess because they had only met the women earlier this evening. Kyle and Kent had sent both men home for the evening after cautioning them to be more careful whom they hooked-up with in the future. But the truth was both women had made it through the club's rigorous screening so he didn't feel they honestly had much room to criticize.

Kelly had refused to admit her mistake and had actually threatened to call the police because Noelle had broken one of her fake fingernails. He and Kent had laughed out loud and asked her how she thought that was going to work out for her when the deputies found out the "nail breaking felon" was one of the county prosecutors. Honestly he was surprised the woman had made it through the membership interview without showing her true colors because she really was a first class bitch.

After long minutes of questioning her, she'd finally

conceded that she had merely pretended to be a sub in order to meet the club's owner. Seems her friends had mentioned he and Kent shared and she was intrigued and wanted to—in her words "hook up with a couple of good looking rich boys for a threesome." Micah had slipped in through the small door at the back of the room and Kyle saw the fury flash in his eyes when he heard her words.

Kyle nodded to Micah, "Get her stuff and escort her off the property. If she doesn't have a ride, call her a taxi and have one of the other guys stay with her until she has been picked up. She doesn't go *anywhere* in this club without an escort. She's done." When he turned back to her, he narrowed his eyes, "It didn't have to be this way, you could have taken your punishment and returned, but your membership is terminated. We will return a pro-rated portion of your membership fee even though we don't have to. We're only doing it because I don't want to run the risk of ever having to deal with you again. And good luck getting into another club because we're on the network with almost every club in the country and we'll be sending this story out far and wide, I assure you."

As Kelly stomped from the room in a huff, Kyle shook his head. Micah turned to him and said, "Hold up on the next interview until I get back" and then walked out. Kyle found the remark interesting and wondered why he had an interest in the young woman sitting in the next room crying. Kyle had been watching her on one of the monitors and she hadn't stopped crying since she'd been led into the room.

Turning to Kent, he asked, "What do you think that is about?"

"No clue. But from what I gathered, those two women hadn't been known to pal around together until tonight. If I were betting, I'd say we have a case of follow the leader. The question is, what are we gonna do with the follower? I'm tempted to give her a second chance and I'm not even sure why."

Kyle agreed and didn't know why either. Maybe Micah could shed some light on the situation. They waited until Micah returned before asking the obvious question. "What's your interest in Mary Dillon?"

Micah didn't back down, just crossed his arms over his chest and smiled. "I have been watching her for a while and almost stepped in when she teamed up with Hagatha this evening. I wish I had, would have probably saved a lot of trouble and sure would have been better for Tobi. Anyway, I think a public punishment and a short suspension might be the best plan. Mary is a follower, I've never seen her be anything but polite to everyone and my guess is, she was only trying to fit in with her new friend. I'm not saying it excuses her behavior, but I think it might explain it. I also think she might be what Ash and Dex are looking for. She is a bit of a pain slut, but seems embarrassed by that."

"You handle the details, because we want to get Tobi upstairs and settled." Kyle tapped the security monitor that covered the reception desk, "Our little subbie is already done." When Kent leaned over and saw Tobi sleeping in the chair his soft curses filled the air.

"I will. If there is a chance to pull this one out, I'd like to try, but ultimately it depends on how this interview goes. I think Ash and Dex are interested, but I'm sure they'll agree that she needs to set this right first." Ash Moore and Dex Raines were two of the most honest men Kyle had ever known and he had complete faith they would make certain Mary atoned for this sin. Chuckling to himself, he wondered if she had any clue just how painful that atonement was likely to be. Both men were strict disciplinarians as Dominants even though it wasn't always apparent when subs first met them. And Micah was even stricter and already seemed to have taken a liking to Tobi, so he'd likely be looking for a bit of retribution when he set up the scene. Kyle shook his head at the whole mess. He'd seen more than one sub safe-word out because she hadn't known the pretty-boy Doms, as Ash and Dex were known, were such hard asses, and he wondered how long the sobbing woman in the next room would last between them.

The interview with Mary hadn't taken long, Micah had been dead on in his assessment of the woman. Kyle hoped she'd be more careful whom she chose to spend time with from now on. Maybe a couple of Doms with a strong hand was what the woman needed and if that was the case, Ash and Dex might well have found a sub. It was ironic because Kyle and Kent had recently discussed the fact they felt several of their friends were waiting to find a permanent sub. They had known Micah was waiting until his buddy was officially discharged next month because the men had often shared women, and they knew Micah didn't want to start without Jax.

They watched as Micah cuffed Mary's hands behind her back and blindfolded her before he started leading her out of their office. Their friend had been the epitome of professional and gruff during her interview but as he was leaving the room, he looked over at them and winked. After the door closed, Kent looked over and grinned. "She isn't going to sit comfortably for a week at least, but I'm sure she'll get one hell of an orgasm outta the deal in the end. Let's wrap up this paperwork and go get our little sub. I don't feel like we're taking particularly good care of her.

Those two drilled her insecurities and now we've left her out there sleeping in a damned chair like an orphan for far too long."

"Agreed, but we need to tie up this paperwork and get the word out about Kelly." They spent the next ten minutes working together and tying things up quickly. Walking out into the reception area, Kyle felt like someone had hit him in the chest with a sledgehammer when he looked down at Tobi. She was so beautiful she took his breath away. Her long lashes fanned out over her cheeks but didn't hide the dark circles under her eyes that were evidence of how totally exhausted she was. She made reference to the fact she didn't live in a particularly safe neighborhood and he wondered how well she'd been sleeping. She was curled on her side with her hands folded under her cheek, and she looked like a sleeping angel surrounded by all those blonde waves of silk. He was grateful that Tank and Regi had covered her with one of the soft subbie blankets because he was sure she'd been flashing everyone in the short dress they'd made her wear.

Kyle thanked Tank and Regi for all they'd done for Tobi, and as he'd expected them to, they both shrugged him off. "Micah will be overseeing the administration of Mary's punishment. After that, she is suspended for thirty days so make a note in her file." He'd seen them both flinch and knew they were thinking the punishment Mary was about to receive wasn't going to be a walk in the park. "Regi, if it's still raining when you close up, please stay in one of the guest cottages. We don't want you driving in this weather." She smiled at him and nodded as he and Kent moved toward Tobi.

Tank surprised them by brushing her hair off her face before they could pick her up. "She is a sweetheart. Hell, before she fell asleep she told me she even likes football. God, she's perfect, just like Regi." Kyle laughed because Regi had rolled her eyes at the big man standing next to her, but she had also leaned over and hugged him. Damn, they really needed to get to work on figuring out how to market Tank's charm.

KENT BENT DOWN, scooped their sleeping beauty up into his arms, and was rewarded when her soft breath brushed against his neck. He knew she hadn't even opened her eyes, but she had sighed his name and he'd leaned down and kissed her forehead. "Yes, sweetness. We're going to take you upstairs now. Go back to sleep, baby." Kent hadn't missed the significance of the fact she had instinctively known he and Kyle apart, and it pleased him more than it probably should have.

They cut through a series of back hallways to avoid the main room because he didn't want Tobi to wake up and see the scene he knew was being played out there. Micah would have made an announcement to the members so anyone who didn't want to watch could move to another part of the club. This was one of the parts of owning a BDSM club that neither he nor his brother liked. They were happy to have an excuse to avoid supervising this punishment, and they damned well didn't want Tobi exposed to it. If she became their sub, they would be very careful what she was allowed to see in the club. Hell, they and all the other male staff members were careful what Regi saw, even if they didn't let the little hellion know they were protecting her.

After Kyle had pressed in the code, the elevator's doors

slid shut and he looked over at Kent and Tobi. "Hello, kitten. Are you enjoying your chariot ride in Kent's arms?" Kent couldn't see her face but it suddenly felt very warm against his neck so he'd bet she was blushing again. *Damn, she just may prove to be the most precious gift mom has ever given us.*

Walking into the large master bath, Kent sat Tobi on the counter and saw her wince. *Christ, I can't believe we left that fucking plug in her for so long. Fucking hell, I'm not sure we deserve her trust.* "I'm sorry, sweetness, we didn't intend for you to wear that plug for so long." Kent heard Kyle's curse from behind him and chuckled because it was obvious his brother had forgotten that particular detail as well.

Tobi looked at him with something between curiosity and concern before inquiring, "What happened to those two women and the men they were supposed to be with? They didn't get in too much trouble did they? I've dealt with their kind for a long time, so I am used to it. Honestly, I probably wouldn't have even mentioned it to you." Kent had to fight back his sudden urge to shake her. *Wouldn't have mentioned it? What the hell?*

Thank heavens Kyle stepped forward and unwrapped the blanket from around her before untying the halter and lifting the dress over her head. "That would have been a huge mistake, kitten. We want to know if anything is bothering you, and that would certainly include being the subject of vindictive words from women who are jealous of our interest in you." He smiled at her slight shiver at being exposed and leaned down and moved her dress aside before circling first one and the other nipple with his tongue. He hummed in satisfaction as he blew small puffs of air over the wet peaks, causing them to draw up even tighter. "Actually we're going to require that kind of 'full disclosure' if you get my drift, kitten." Kyle laid her down on the counter. "Pull your legs up and apart."

Kent started the water in the shower and then stepped back to help her get into position. At his nod, Kyle sealed his lips over Tobi's. Kent knew the kiss was a distraction and quickly took advantage of the opportunity to pull the plug from her tender rear hole and set it aside to clean later. "Come on, sweetness, the warm water will be good for your sore muscles. Sleeping in that chair couldn't have been comfortable for you."

Tobi's soft moans of delight as the warm water slid over her tired muscles were quickly making both Kent and Kyle hard. And when her dainty little hands slid up their bare chests they both groaned. "You promised…you aren't going to back out because of those two women are you?" Kent was pleased that she'd given up finding out what had taken place in regards to those two, but he doubted the subject would stay dead and buried indefinitely.

"No way, baby. You are much too fuckable to ignore. But let us take care of you a bit first, alright? Not everything went like we'd planned tonight and a part of our need to care for you is as much for our own benefit as it is for you—so indulge us a bit, okay?" Kent felt her muscles relaxing beneath his hands as he kneaded her shoulders. He moved her toward the glass wall and pressed her against it. Her gasp when her nipples made contact with the cool glass made him smile. "What's the matter, sweetness?"

"Nothing, just a bit of a surprise. But your hands are working magic on my back. I'm worried about melting into a puddle of goo. Oh God!" Kent smiled at her reaction when he'd pressed himself against her backside. He'd pressed his rigid length into the crack of her ass as he slid his hand around in front of her. He used one arm to wrap around her waist and anchor her to his chest while the other hand slid between the slick folds of her sex. Sliding his fingers through her heat as the warm water pulsed around them was beyond erotic. Tobi didn't seem to have any inkling of how truly sensual she was and that genuineness was a magnet to everyone who met her.

"How does that feel, sweetness? Tell me what it feels like when I tease your clit."

The words, in her whispered breath, stole his control. "Please, Sir, I need you." Kent forgot that he'd demanded she tell him how it felt. Hell, he probably wouldn't have been able to tell you his own name. His entire body was drowning in his desperate desire to sink deep inside her. Kyle handed him a small packet and Kent groaned in relief. Tearing the package apart using his teeth, Kent quickly sheathed himself and pushed her legs apart with his thigh. "Arch your back just a bit and let me in. I wanted to wait but I can't—I want you too desperately." Her instant compliance was all the permission he needed and he slid in fast and deep. Leaning forward so his mouth was pressed against her ear, Kent just breathed her in for several seconds. The walls of her vagina were flexing and rippling around him and he needed several seconds for them both to adjust. "Fuck me. You are so tight. And your body is surrounding me with a heat that is nearly scorching in its intensity, sweetness. You have unraveled every bit of my control."

"No. Please. Master. No control. I need you to make me forget my fears. I want this…I need this." Tobi's words were gasped out and the perfect spark to the explosive need Kent had been trying to hold back. Every bit of his consciousness was overtaken by a relentless yearning to fuck the woman in his arms hard and fast, and any effort he had been making to hold back evaporated to join the steam surrounding them.

"Hang on, sweet girl, because this is going to be fast and furious. I promise slow and sweet—next time." There just weren't any more words to say, well at least none more important than finding his pleasure inside his woman. Sliding in and out of her lush body and making sure she was enjoying it as much as he was became his entire reason for living at this moment. Everything—every soft sigh, every gentle touch, every electrical impulse that raced up his spine before settling in his testicles was centered in this woman's satisfaction. He felt her body shudder just before she came apart. He managed two more strokes before he followed her over the edge of a canyon that was filled to the brim with sweet ecstasy.

A part of Kent's soul knew he'd just made a lifetime connection, but it was standing a long way behind the part that was singing the Halleluiah Chorus like a gospel singer in tent revival-mode. Tobi's scream when she'd found her own release was still echoing off the tiled walls of the shower and Kent was thrilled he'd managed to outlast her, even if it had only been by mere seconds. "Sweetness, you undo me."

The truth was he felt like he'd been run over by a truck loaded with bricks. She had leveled him once again with a single orgasm. He was worried his knees were going to fold and he didn't want to take her to the floor with him. He turned and was grateful to see Kyle standing close ready to take her into his arms. "Come here, kitten, I want to get you washed and into bed before I succumb to the same fate as my brother and risk us all drowning in this shower." Kent felt himself chuckle, which was a miracle because right at this moment he couldn't even feel his damned toes because his entire body felt like he'd been hit by a lightning bolt.

Chapter Ten

WATCHING KENT FUCK Tobi with wild abandon in the shower had mesmerized Kyle. He'd stood rooted in place and had barely been able to breathe. Holy hell, he hadn't even wanted to blink for fear he'd miss some small detail of the pleasure he saw moving through her ever-changing expressions. The sweet sounds she made alone had almost made him take his cock in his own hand. When she'd finally let go at Kent's command, Kyle's knees had almost folded. Thank God her scream had bounced around the tiled enclosure and jarred him back into the moment. He'd tease her about that later because he wasn't sure any of them would ever hear quite right again.

Seeing how devastated Kent looked had made him smile also because his brother had a reputation among subs for always being the last Dom standing. Pulling her sated body against his had felt perfect and he quickly pressed his lips against her ear and whispered words of encouragement and praise because he knew Kent would have done it, but right now his brother seemed to be fighting to just stay upright.

Kyle made short work of shampooing and conditioning her long hair before using the sweet-smelling shower gel that Regi had sent up for her earlier. By the time he was ready to rub his hands over every inch of her delectable body she had recovered enough to stand on her own. He was grateful because it allowed him a much better view of the landscape his hands were currently mapping in exquisite detail. The bubbles from the soap ran in sexy rivers around the curves of her breasts as they slid toward her pussy where they disappeared into the same sweet spot he wanted to shove his cock, which was bobbing in enthusiasm. "You are so beautiful, kitten. And it's a beauty that radiates from your core all the way up to the surface. Watching you charm each and every person that you met this evening kept Kent and I both completely entranced. We couldn't keep our eyes off you. I've never walked through the club and not cared about a single thing that was happening around me, but it happened over and over tonight. Nothing mattered but you, and seeing the shattered look on your face when Noelle led you out of the lounge made me heartsick." If she was theirs, Kyle vowed he'd spend his life trying to prevent that expression from ever crossing her face again. The disillusionment had made her usually vibrant green eyes a dull moss color that was devoid of the light that usually sparkled all around her.

"I'm sorry. I really shouldn't let those things get to me because by reacting I'm giving power to their words, but they seemed to zero in on the worst of my fears. I've always been amazed at how cruel women can be to one another in the midst of all their chatter about sisterhood and all that phony-baloney stuff." Kyle couldn't agree more, he'd often wondered how women could profess to support one another all the while they were undermining the efforts of their family, friends, and colleagues.

"Don't ever apologize for the way you feel, kitten. Our hope is that over time you'll become confident enough to confront those situations head-on. But until then never doubt that we have your back, okay?" He rinsed her thoroughly and pulled her out of the shower so he could blot her glowing skin dry with a bath sheet. Kyle had always loved the post-orgasmic flush that no woman could begin to fake. It was just one of the ways a Dom could always tell when a sub was trying to force their own response or was just out-and-out faking a release she hadn't had. Tobi was positively glowing and it made her even more beautiful.

He'd seen Doms come completely apart at the seams if a sub they were scening with tried to fake an orgasm. Kyle had looked on as Micah had risked his cover while they had been on a mission in Germany so he could rescue a sub that was being whipped by her Master for faking an orgasm. The sub had been so frightened of the sadist that she would have never been able to find a sexual release. The Dom had been relentless because he'd had an audience and he couldn't find his way around his own ego to provide the woman what she had needed in order to come.

Micah's dad had been career Air Force and they'd lived all over the world so his German was nearly as good as his English...and French...and Italian. He had been able to intercede without causing too much of an incident and after buying the man a few drinks, Micah had managed to make him forget all about the woman whose friends had quickly hustled her away from the club. During late night bullshit sessions over beer and pizza, the three of them had often wondered what had become of that traumatized young woman. Kyle hoped she had been able to find a safe, sane, and consensual way to continue playing if that was what it took to fulfill her sexually. But he seriously doubted she'd ever been brave enough to try again.

Kyle had let Tobi comb out and dry her hair while he lit candles in the bedroom and turned down the bed. What

Kent had given her in the shower helped to take the edge off for her, and he hoped that would help her relax and enjoy being made love to in a way that would bind the other half of her sexuality to them. One of the things their dads had told them about women was that you had to feed both sides of their needs. Kyle remembered Dad Dean's words, "Women are much more complicated and interesting than we are. Their sexuality is multi-faceted and always evolving. If you want to satisfy a woman you need to touch her mind *and* her body, because either one alone isn't enough."

Over the years Kyle had come to appreciate that advice more and more, and he had a feeling it was about to become some of the most valuable help he'd ever been given about women. By the time Tobi was finished, Kent had dried and they walked out of the bathroom together. The sight of her walking naked with her skin still dewy from her shower and her hair flowing all around her shoulders was breathtaking. With the light from all the candles he'd lit reflecting off the lightest shades of her hair, she looked like she was surrounded by a halo of glowing light befitting an angel. "Jesus, Joseph, and Mary, you are so beautiful I have trouble forming words because my brain is short circuiting." He held open his arms and was pleased when she walked directly into his embrace.

Kyle just held her in his arms for long seconds until he could feel her relaxing into his embrace. She felt perfect against him despite the large disparity in their heights. He let his hands caress slow circles over her back and smiled when she moaned in pleasure. Leaning down, he picked her up and walked to the bed, placing her in the center before lying down alongside her. He used the tip of one finger to trace lazy nonsensical designs over her torso and smiled when her nipples tightened into sharp points and goose bumps raced over her ivory skin. "You are so responsive and that's a gift to your Doms, you know, because it's a sign of the trust you've given us." He let her consider his words because he wanted her to realize the significance of what he was saying. It didn't matter they had known each other less than twenty-four hours, her soul recognized and accepted them or they couldn't have established this level of trust so soon.

"I don't understand it, because I'm really not usually like this." Her voice was quiet and he didn't like that she was questioning herself.

"Like what, kitten? You don't usually trust this easily? Or perhaps you meant you don't usually sleep in the nude? Or were you referring to something we already know about you?" At her wide-eyed response, he knew he had been right.

"Well, I don't usually sleep with men I have just met and I've certainly never been in bed with two men at the same time, that's for sure." Kyle knew Tobi was trying to lighten the mood, but he also heard the underlying insecurity in her words and tone. She was worried she was presenting herself badly to both he and his brother, and even though he understood what she was saying—hell, he even understood why she might think that considering society's double standard in how they view men's and women's sexual experience. But that didn't mean he was going to ignore the problem either.

"Kitten, we feel a special connection to you and I think you feel that also. You admitted to an interest in BDSM so let's explore that this weekend. We know full well you do not usually sleep with men you have just met, but one of the things you should understand about the people in this lifestyle is they usually have spent enough time being trained, whether they are a Dominant or a submissive, they know exactly what they want. And that training helps them recognize what's *right* for them when it appears front and center—even in a blinding thunderstorm.

He could see her eyes had gone glassy with unshed tears and Kyle didn't speak for a couple of minutes because he wanted her to have a chance to work through what he'd said and pull herself back from the edge. Empowering a woman, helping her reach every success she could possibly reach, was what all three of their parents had always stressed as one of the most crucial elements of any long-term relationship's success.

Kyle planned to talk with Kent tomorrow morning during their early morning workout, because unless he was missing his guess, her current job was as dead-end as they came. With the plans they'd been looking over for adding on a retail pavilion of small shops, Tobi's design and marketing skills would be a perfect fit. He knew he was getting way ahead of himself, but he wanted to start mapping out a plan because everything about this situation seemed perfect.

"The time for thinking is over, kitten. Now it's time for pleasure." Leaning over her, he pressed butterfly kisses over her eyelids, "Close your eyes and let yourself sink into the sensations. I'm going to use this silk scarf as a blindfold because I want you to concentrate on what you are feeling as each touch moves over you. Notice how your body responds to the different ways we can bring you pleasure. Your other senses will become enhanced since you won't be continually looking for visual clues. You're a very visual person, I see it in your eyes because they are constantly assessing and evaluating your environment. And that is an amazing skill, just not one I want you to utilize right now." He was pleased when she closed her eyes and kept them closed. The small smile that tugged at her bow-shaped mouth let him know he'd been right about her being visually driven. He and Kent would work to enhance all of her senses, but tonight he wanted to start with touch.

"Spread your legs apart, kitten." She spread them apart but just barely. He and Kent both chuckled softly. "Well, that was a good start. Here, let us help." He placed his hand on the inside of one knee and his brother placed his palm on the other and they moved her legs as far apart as they could without putting too much strain on her tired muscles. He felt her shiver as the cool air hit her bare pussy and he loved watching her nipples react as well. "Beautiful, kitten. Did you notice that when the air hit your bare pussy lips the sensation traveled from your sex up to your pretty pink nipples? That is the kind of sensation we want you to note because it is a clear indicator of what a truly sensual woman you are."

Kyle was intentionally using a measured cadence in his words because he understood the power of the human voice to seduce. Tobi had a strong sensual side even if she hadn't fully integrated it with the intelligent career woman she'd worked so hard to become. Sure, she was going along with their request to stay the weekend because she had a deep curiosity about the lifestyle, but come Sunday night he was worried "Career Tobi" would return in full force.

The best he could hope for was to establish enough of a foundation of trust that she would feel comfortable returning and letting them visit her in Austin. Even though it wasn't a great distance to travel, it wasn't a trip they would be able to make every day either, so the sooner they could move past that stage the better he would like it.

Tobi's acknowledgement of the connection brought him back to the moment and he chided himself for becoming distracted. The beautiful woman before him deserved every bit of his attention and she was going to get it—in spades. "Kitten, your pussy is nicely swollen and a lovely shade of red. I can hardly wait to slide in so deep we feel like we've become one. But first, I want to make sure you are ready and that means you have to come again—at least once."

Tobi's body stiffened, "Oh God, I'm not sure I'm going to survive this."

"Oh, sweet kitten, you are not only going to survive, but you'll flourish I promise you." Kyle took the soft feather Kent handed him and drew broad painting strokes around her breasts, careful to avoid the areolas and nipples but enjoying watching them tighten in response. When he trailed the soft interior vane of the large feather he was using down her midline the muscles under her abdomen quivered. Leaning over her, he drew circles around her navel with his tongue as she groaned and started to try to lift into his touch. Kent helped press her back to the mattress and Kyle spoke against her ear, "Stay still and let me play a bit." He was pleased that she was shaved but if she became theirs, they would have her waxed so she didn't have to bother with it every day. Maybe they'd make room in the pavilion for on-site spa services.

By the time he had moved his tongue in a hot trail all the way to her pussy, her honey-coated labia was almost pulsing with need. Kyle ran the tip of his tongue around her clit and watched the little bundle of nerves push even further from its protective hood. He paused just long enough that he knew she'd had a chance to regain some of her control before he blew a puff of air over her clit and immediately sucked it in and pressed down on the tight bud with his teeth. Tobi's scream was long and high-pitched and as she arched so strongly, she pushed out of Kent's hold. Every muscle in her body seemed to seize at the exact same moment, her body seemed to light up from the inside as she let the waves of pleasure work their way through her.

Tobi's chanted pleas to various divinities made him smile as he moved up between her legs. He quickly rolled on the condom that his brother handed him and just as he started to slowly push inside her still vibrating vagina, he pushed the blindfold off and watched as she blinked, her eyes were the deep emerald he'd noticed they became when she was aroused. It took her a few seconds to adjust to the dim lights but the color had remained the same. "I want to see your eyes as I enter you, kitten. And I want you to see mine so you know how much I want you." Kyle pushed in slowly giving her swollen tissues time to adjust to his invasion. "Fuck. You are so hot and tight. Damn, I want to make this last so we are going to go slowly. No, baby, please don't tighten down on me, my control is already hanging precariously by nothing but the finest of threads."

Continuing his slow quest for entrance, Kyle pressed forward in fractions of an inch before pulling back. He continued to make slow progress and never let his eyes stray from hers. Watching her eyes darken and dilate further with desire until her pupils were surrounded by a narrow ring of moss green was incredible to watch. He felt her heart pounding against her chest and the small mewing sounds she was making were about to slingshot him into the stratosphere. When he felt the tip of his penis press against her cervix Tobi's moan felt like a choir of angels had burst into song. "Does that feel good, kitten? Do you like knowing I'm shoved inside you as far as I can go?"

"Oh God, you feel so hot inside me. It feels like you are trying to burn me up from the inside out and my body is all too willing to comply. Hell, every cell in my body has turned mutinous and it wants to steal my control. I can feel every ridge of your cock as it presses inside me. I loved Master Kent's fast and furious, but I love this too. How can that be? I don't understand, but I don't want to waste a second of this feeling thinking about it either."

Kyle tried to hold back, but her words had been all it took to shatter all of his illusions of control and send them hurtling into space. He set a steady but pounding rhythm and slid his arms under her knees so her legs were draped over his elbows. He knew the slight shift in position had worked perfectly when he shoved deep and she started gasping and begging for more. Kyle was sure she didn't realize she was pleading and if she did, she probably didn't even know what it was that she needed. The spongy spot his cock was caressing with every stroke was precisely what he'd been aiming for because he was determined they were going to come together.

"Please, Master, oh please, I have to come, please let me come." Tobi's desperation not to come until she'd been told to was a testament to her submissiveness.

Kent smiled at him because they both knew he hadn't told her to wait for permission, and the fact she'd already referred to them both as Master spoke volumes about how perfect she was for them. Being a submissive was truly at the very heart of her personality and he wondered if she had any idea what a big part of her had been missing. He knew she was on the cusp of losing the battle to hold back and he didn't want her to feel as if she'd failed, so he leaned down and whispered, "Come for me, kitten."

Tobi's reaction to his command was so quick he had barely managed to seal his lips over hers when her scream filled is mouth. He loved feeling the vibrations of her voice moving through his own mouth as he caught her vocal release. Kyle traced every inch of her sweet mouth with his tongue before increasing the thrusts of his hips as he drove in and out of her relentlessly. He'd felt her sweet cream coating his cock as she'd come and he loved the wet sounds their bodies were making as he made love to her. When the fire in his balls began streaking up his spine before it plummeted back down to his cock, Kyle moved his mouth to her ear, bit down on the lobe, and growled, "Again." She didn't disappoint him because just as the kaleidoscope of colors lit up the world around him, he felt her channel tightening down like a vice once again.

The climax that slammed into him was the most intense experience of Kyle's life and when he was finally able to pull in gasping breaths, he realized he was pressing Tobi into the mattress. *Fuck, she'll never be able to breath with me laying on top of her.* Struggling to roll to the side, he kept his arms wrapped tightly around her so she was pressed flush against his chest. "Kitten, are you alright?"

"Honestly? I have no idea. My entire body feels like it's covered in those sparklers we all had as little kids. Everything is still tingling." She sounded as spent as he felt and letting her go so he could take care of the condom was one of the hardest things he'd ever done. Now he understood the look he'd seen on Kent's face earlier after their interlude in the shower. Kyle felt as if he'd been totally destroyed and then put back together too quickly, and now there were still some pieces that hadn't yet been returned to their rightful places.

TOBI WASN'T SURE if she would ever be able to walk again. Kyle had literally turned her into a big pile of goo and all she could do was lay limp as he pulled away and Kent rolled her so he was holding her against his chest. She could still feel her heart pounding and her body was shaking but she didn't understand why. "What are you thinking about so hard, sweetness? I can almost hear the wheels of that sharp mind of yours spinning round and round." Tobi could hear the amusement in Kent's tone and even though it seemed to take a monumental effort, she managed to smile.

When she tried to speak all she could do was squeak out the words and the shaking seemed to be getting worse. "Shaking. Why?" was all she could manage to push past her dry lips. Just then Kyle reappeared with a warm rag and a bottle of water, which he handed to Kent.

"Here, drink this first and then we'll talk after Kyle cleans you up. But so you'll stop worrying, the shaking is perfectly normal. It's a reaction to the extreme isometric tension of your muscles during your release. And the short story is that it's proof of the intensity of your climax."

As she was considering his explanation, she felt Kyle move between her legs and start to clean her sex. Jerking to try to sit up while pulling her legs tightly together, she said, "Oh God, no, please, I can do that." But her efforts were cut off quickly by Kent's enormous hand splayed over her chest as he pushed her back against the pillow and Kyle's hands manacled her ankles and pulled her legs back apart.

"Kitten, I'm perfectly aware that you can do this, but it's my responsibility, privilege, and pleasure to do it for you." He went back to work cleaning her before patting her tender tissues dry with an even softer towel as he kept speaking, "Consider this. You have put yourself in our care for the weekend and we take that very seriously. Your trust is a precious gift and we won't abuse it or devalue it by not holding up our end of the bargain. This is a time for me to pamper you and also check for injuries or signs of bruising. Those things would require additional attention and you wouldn't be able to see the area as easily as I can. Do you understand?"

Tobi hadn't considered those things and hadn't run across that in any of the research she'd done either. But then, most of what she'd seen had been scary and she had been close to deciding there wasn't anything in the lifestyle for her when she'd come on a couple of e-books that had stressed the romantic side of BDSM. She'd read the stories and they had rekindled her interest and given her hope that this might be what she had felt was missing in her previous sexual experience. "Yes, I do understand. And thank you for taking time to explain it to me." She hadn't really known what else to say, after all it wasn't like she could say some of the crazy things bouncing around in her head. *Hey, thanks for giving my pussy a first class pounding and then checking it for damage. Lord love a leper this is a whole new level of flocked-up, even for me.* She jumped when Kent's bark of laughter jolted her into the realization that she'd spoken the words aloud…again. Closing her eyes and groaning, she asked, "I didn't say that out loud did I? Oh God, please say no."

"You know, sweetness, I'm not sure which is more amusing—your tour guide chatter during the mental field trips you seem to favor or the look on my brother's face." Tobi was certain that Kent's teasing was as much to get

Kyle to lighten up as it was to gently point out her error, but from the look on Kyle's face, she didn't think it had been very effective.

"Kitten, there are several problems with what you just said. First, your mindset is not right or you wouldn't have even been thinking that. Don't forget that a submissive's duty is to please their Dom and since it *pleases me* to care for you, that should have been the end of it. Secondly, I take exception to your crass rewording of what I'd explained to you and you had *pretended* to accept. Third, you misled me to believe that you had accepted information I'd given you in all sincerity. And finally, you are too bright and beautiful to curse and substituting in words will not count as acceptable. That was four issues and I'm going to give you four swats, but rest assured you are getting off very easy. This isn't how I wanted this to end tonight, but you've left me no choice, because you are better than this behavior, kitten. You wanted to learn about the D/s lifestyle and I assure you this is only the tip of the iceberg."

She noticed he'd moved so he was now sitting on the edge of the bed and she had a flash of panic, not from any kind of fear of being spanked because the truth was the idea was kicking her arousal into high gear once again. No, this panic was pure fear of rejection. She spent all of her time trying so hard to please everyone else that she inevitably ended up messing things up. When she looked up he was watching her and he just continued to study her for long moments before asking, "Do you want to use your safe word, kitten?"

Tobi already felt the tears starting to burn the backs of her eyes as she shook her head back and forth before remembering that she had to speak her answers. "No, Sir."

"Come here, kitten, and lay over my lap." Kent helped

her sit up and she crawled over the bed and put herself over Kyle's knees so her feet were still touching the floor, but he easily shifted her position. When he'd finished, her ass was peaked and no doubt positioned in perfect alignment for his hand to land on her padded flesh. Her feet weren't touching the ground, which meant the only thing keeping her from falling off his knees was his left arm wrapped around her torso. She'd been beaten every time her father had come home drunk after her mother died so she didn't fear the pain, but knowing she had disappointed him made her heartsick.

She hadn't been prepared for the first slap because her mind had been wandering through the trenches of her childhood so she hadn't been able to hold back the gasp. "I'm sorry." She had gasped the words because her father had always added strokes if she made noise and didn't immediately apologize. The rest of the swats came quickly and didn't hurt as much because she'd been mentally prepared. When he was finished, Tobi had instinctively put her hands out so she'd be ready when he shoved her from his lap, but he had just used his hand to massage her stinging ass cheeks and then slid his fingers through her folds. And even though she was damp, she was far from wet.

"Kitten, you were aroused by the idea of me spanking you when I first mentioned it, but then everything changed—why? I'll caution you that you already know lying, even if it's only by omission or editing, is not allowed. And kitten, you are in a pretty vulnerable position to take any risks." She wasn't sure, but it almost sounded like he'd been amused at his own words.

"I...um, I remembered when my dad...well, that was a pretty bad time in my life." Those were the only words she got out before he lifted her and turned her so she was once again sitting on the bed. She immediately used her heels to slide toward the end of the bed. It was time to face the fact she'd blown her chance and move on down the road. Not only was she going to end up unemployed, but she'd just managed to blow the chance to spend time with the two hottest guys she'd ever known.

Kyle's hand wrapped around her ankle and stilled her movements. "Where do you think you are going, kitten? Do you really think you were going to get away with that lame-assed explanation? Or that we'd be finished with you just because you got four swats that obviously triggered some awfully unpleasant memories?" She didn't answer his questions, but just blinked frantically trying to stem the flood of tears that was building up faster than she could hold them back. Tobi felt like that little Dutch boy with his finger in the dam as the wall cracks all around him and the water washed over him despite his best effort to hold it back. She didn't even realize she was crying until she heard his muttered, "Fuck" as he picked her up and moved to sit on the bed. Leaning against the headboard, she felt Kent pull her feet into his lap.

BY THE TIME Kyle had realized things had gone south with Tobi's spanking they were so far gone he could have sworn he'd seen a fucking penguin waddle through the room. When she mentioned her dad, it had answered one question, but raised ten more. He'd spanked a lot of subs and he knew for a fact many of those had been disciplined in the same way by one or both of their parents. But it was the subs who'd been abused that had often had the strongest mixed reaction. They were often aroused when they were told they'd be spanked by their Dom, but there was a point during the punishment where their mind switched back and everything changed. He knew he and Kent would do all they could to help her work through the issues, but they'd need a lot more information before they could figure out how to proceed.

When he'd settled her on his lap sitting next to Kent, she'd been sobbing so hard all they could do was hold her and wait for the flood of emotion to wear itself out and pass. He'd almost stopped when she'd gasped after the first swat and apologized because he'd gotten the feeling she was apologizing for making the sound rather than what she was being punished for. And then when she'd become completely stoic during the rest of the spanking, he'd been sure that had been the case. He'd guess she'd been punished for making any noise while she'd been spanked as a kid and if his instincts were right, it had happened often and had been a lot more severe than what she'd just experienced under his hand. Kissing the top of her head, he just kept whispering words of encouragement and assuring her that it was perfectly fine to get it all out.

The third time she'd tried to get off his lap he'd finally had enough. "Tobi, stop trying to get off my lap. Why do you continue to think that is going to work?"

Her eyes were red and swollen from her crying jag, but it was the desolation in them that tore at his heart. "I let you down" was all she was able to stutter out between gasps, but it was enough to render him completely speechless. *She thinks we're so disappointed in her because she made a couple of mistakes that we'd send her away? Christ, what kind of childhood did this woman have? And where are the people responsible?*

Kent was gently smoothing the tears from her cheeks with his thumbs and smiling at her. His brother's actions reminded Kyle of why they had always intended to share a woman. Not only had they known the pleasure would be exponentially better, but also from what they'd seen at home, it took two men to keep up with the kind of woman they'd be attracted to. God knew it took both of their dads to keep up with their hell-on-wheels mama sometimes. "Sweetness, did you think we'd wash our hands of you just because you got a paddlin'? Because I gotta tell ya, that is probably just the first of many you're going to get. And those swats were to help you learn a lesson. If we had been going to send you down the road, baby, we wouldn't have bothered to correct the behavior, now would we?"

Kyle could tell by the wide-eyed look she was giving Kent she hadn't even considered that possibility. Leaning forward, he kissed her temple, "Kitten, it would have been much easier to just ignore the whole thing and then quietly wave good-bye to you tomorrow. But we want you to be the best you can be. You already knew that your attitude and words weren't right or you wouldn't have looked so worried when you realized you had said them aloud. What kind of message would we have sent if we'd simply ignored that? Would you have believed that we were really trying to show you what this lifestyle is about?"

Tobi was chewing on her bottom lip and Kyle had to fight his smile as he watched her process everything he'd said. "No, I don't think I would have although I might not have known why."

Kent moved his hands in gentle massaging strokes up and down Tobi's calves. "Sweetness, that is why it is our job to lead. We promised to teach you and that is exactly what this has been about—not our burning desire to control your every thought and emotion—but it's about us helping you grow and find the happiness I think you have probably found very elusive. Until somebody steps up and shows you how much you are valued, it doesn't matter how much they tell you. We will always use words to correct your thinking or behavior, but we'll always back up what we said with what we would do. Sometimes that will work to your advantage and there will be other times that you won't feel that way." Kent grinned at her before continuing, "But you will *always* know you can depend on us and that our word is golden."

Kyle was pleased Kent had managed to explain one of BDSM's guiding principles and had applied it perfectly in this situation. Because Tobi's mind was sharp and obviously moved at the speed of light, he was sure she hadn't missed any of the myriad of implications either. Kyle watched as she seemed to relax within the span of the few deep breaths she took. "Now, we need to rest. We are all exhausted and if we're going to enjoy our time together tomorrow, we need to get some sleep."

Settling her between them, Kyle couldn't help but notice how perfectly she seemed to fit. It was as if she'd been made just for them. Both he and Kent had given her sweet good night kisses and smiled at her soft sighs before he heard her breathing even out and knew she'd already fallen asleep. The dark circles under eyes were even more pronounced now and that was something they would need to watch closely. They needed to make a concerted effort to see to it that she got enough rest so those faded until they were just an unpleasant memory of a time when her life hadn't included men who loved and cared for her.

Chapter Eleven

KENT WASN'T SURE exactly what had woken him up, but the pink shade of the light filtering in around the edges of the bedroom draperies told him he hadn't been asleep nearly long enough. Glancing over at his phone, which he'd left on the nightstand, he saw the blinking message light. Since he didn't really use the phone for anything but Prairie Winds business, it was likely from a member of their staff. Easing himself out from under Tobi, he immediately missed her warmth and kissed her forehead when she stirred. "Go back to sleep, sweetness. I'll be back in a minute." She smiled without ever opening her eyes and then quickly slid back into sleep.

Moving out into the hall, Kent checked the messages and silently cursed. He padded down the hall to his bedroom and grabbed a pair of sweats and a t-shirt before heading to the small office they'd set up in the apartment. When Micah answered all Kent said was "Talk to me." One of the great things about employing other vets on their security team was their understanding of his and Kyle's brusque communication style.

"When I saw Tobi's name on the schedule for your interview I plugged her into our system. We got a hit on her address earlier this evening, it came in from the Austin P.D. After making a few calls, I drove into the city to find out firsthand what was going on. I'm at the scene now and it's not good, buddy. Somebody torched her tiny apartment. I'll pull out what I can, but it isn't going to be much. What do you want me to do with anything I save?" Kent sighed, even though he was thrilled to have an excuse to move Tobi onto their compound, he knew this was going to hurt her and that was the last thing he wanted.

"Bring it here. I'm not going to wake her unless we absolutely have to. She was beyond exhausted when we finally got her settled in. Have you talked to any of her neighbors?"

"Yeah and there is a spit-fire Latino woman who lives across the hall that almost crawled up my ass when I started asking questions of Tobi's neighbors who had gathered around." Kent could hear him chuckling. "Damn I think you need to hire her. Talk about a *take no prisoners* attitude in a gorgeous package. Anyway, I hope it's all right that I assured her Tobi was in a safe place. I promised her that Tobi would call and check in tomorrow morning. Her name is Gracie—go figure." Kent didn't miss the amusement or the interest in his friend's voice.

"That's fine and if she needs a place to stay I think the back guest house is ready to go. She's obviously a friend of Tobi's. Will the Fire Marshall let everyone stay in place?"

"Probably, even though in truth no one should have been living in the damned building even before this fire. The super told me the entire complex is set to be torn down in a couple of months anyway and that all the tenants were notified this morning they have thirty days to vacate. He asked me to pass along the message to Tobi because he hadn't seen her yet to tell her. This place is in a very dangerous part of town, man. I'm glad your girl isn't coming back here." For Micah to refer to the place as unsafe was telling. They'd all been in places rejected for the

Dante's Seven Levels of Hell, so having him describe the area as dangerous sent a chill up Kent's spine.

"Make sure you leave your card with Gracie if you can't get her to come with you. And give her my personal guarantee that Tobi is fine and will call her first thing in the morning. I assume you got her number—just in case." He couldn't hold back the amusement in his voice as he asked the question he already knew the answer to.

"As a matter of fact I did." Micah's chuckle told Kent he'd been right. "Jax will be home next week and she is just sassy enough to be his type. I need to get back over there and see what I can salvage for your girl. I'll take it down to the shop because I'm sure it's going to reek of smoke." Kent was certain Micah was right and there was no reason to bring that into the garage or any part of the club.

Leaning back in his large leather office chair, he propped his feet up on the edge of his desk and looked out into the slowly waking countryside. Ordinarily he loved this time of the morning. It had always given him a sense of peace and he'd liked sharing coffee with his mom before anyone else had gotten up. Kent knew he'd gotten his love of mornings from all the heart to heart chats they'd shared while watching the first rays of sunshine light up the colorful east Texas sky. He was lost in thought and didn't realize he was no longer alone until he saw Tobi's reflection in the glass. She had put on one of their dress shirts and her hair was a riot of waves and curls, and she was the most beautiful women he had ever seen.

As she walked toward him, he put his hand out over the edge of his chair and she placed her cool fingers in his. "Come here, sweetness. Are you cold?" He pulled her on his lap and she curled into a ball and snuggled against him like a sweet kitten.

"Not really, but I woke up and you were gone and I got worried." He knew she hadn't been worried for his safety so he was pretty sure he understood what her worry had been about.

"Well, love, I saw a message on my phone that needed attention, and I didn't want to disturb you so I came down here to return the call." Kent hadn't said it was anything for her to worry about because that wasn't the truth and he didn't plan to lie to her, but he would like to delay telling her if he could get her to rest a bit more. The impact of bad news always seemed to be compounded when you were tired and she'd been running on empty before she'd fallen asleep earlier.

Kent wasn't surprised to see Kyle walk in a few minutes later, but the steaming mug of coffee he held was certainly an unexpected pleasure. Kyle grabbed the soft throw from the sofa on the other side of the office and tucked it around Tobi. "I woke up when you left the room and hoped she'd stay sleeping but as you see..." Kyle nodded toward the angel sleeping once again now that she was safely tucked in his arms and smiled.

"Yeah, she actually got the drop on me, I didn't hear her come in. I didn't know she was there until I saw her reflection in the window, which tells you how distracted I was." There were some habits he'd learned as a SEAL that he'd hoped to keep for a lifetime because they'd saved his life more than once. Chief among those was being vigilantly aware of his surroundings. Sighing to himself, he wondered if he'd become so blasé that he was already forgetting the fact they'd made a lot of powerful enemies over the years or had he just been too lost in his thoughts of Tobi? Shrugging it off, he turned to Kyle, "We've got a problem. I just got off the phone with Micah."

Kent glanced down at Tobi and saw she was blinking up at him with sleepy eyes. *Damn.* He hadn't meant to wake her, but figured he might as well get this over with. Pressing a kiss to her forehead, he continued, "I'm sorry, sweetness, but I have some bad news. It seems there was a fire in your apartment earlier this evening." When she started struggling to sit up, he tightened his hold. "Hold still and listen a minute, love. Let me tell you what I know." By the time he'd finished relating his conversation with Micah, minus the parts about Jax and Gracie, Tobi's face was pressed against his neck and he could feel her tears against his bare skin.

For several minutes none of them said anything. The set of Kyle's jaw told Kent his brother was livid that someone had tried to hurt Tobi. Kent felt the same way, but adding anger to the emotions surrounding her right now certainly wouldn't do anything to help the situation. Kent watched Kyle stabbing at the keys of his phone and imagined he was alerting all of their staff to the fact they needed to be particularly mindful of all the club's security protocols and to contact one of them with any questions. Despite the early hour, both of their phones started lighting up like Rockefeller Center at Christmas almost immediately. Kent appreciated the fact their people were diligent and had acknowledged the message and promised to do their part to keep Tobi safe. But right now, the woman in his arms was in serious need of some attention.

TOBI THOUGHT HER heart was going to stop beating as she listened to Kent tell she and Kyle about the fire in her apartment. She wondered if there would be anything left for her to salvage, it wasn't like she'd had too much to begin with, and now she was grateful her brother had recently taken all their family photos so he could scan them. The first thing she needed to do was get to a thrift store to get some clothes. When she remembered that she'd also lost her car she finally let the sadness that had been threatening to bubble to the surface wash over her. *Damn it to hell. She'd finally become the total failure her dad had always predicted she would. How could so much bad happen so quickly?*

Taking a deep breath, she looked up and saw both men looking at her. "Do you think you could maybe…give me a ride to a thrift store to get some clothes? I could call my brother when I am finished and he could come pick me up. That way you wouldn't have to drive me to the other side of town." She felt Kent stiffen beneath her and when she looked at Kyle all she saw was fury. *Well, seems that option is off the table.* "Look, don't worry about it, okay? I'll just call Ricky"

Kent had cut her off by demanding, "Who is Ricky?" Wow, she could almost feel the possessiveness coming off him in waves. There was a small piece of her that was pleased by that, even if she shouldn't be.

"Ricky is my brother. I don't have a car or clothes. Crap on a cracker, I don't have anything except those two bags of drenched things from my car. He is the only family I have, so I have to call him even though he's going to blame me for being in this pickle." Her brother had always been the perfect child. Perfect grades. Perfect appearance. Perfect profession. Perfect wife. Blah. It was enough to make her gag and the thought of being told several times a day for the next few months what a burden she was, well…that wasn't something she was particularly looking forward to either.

When she realized she'd drifted off into her own thoughts again she looked up to see Kyle shaking his head. "If we paddle her every time she does that, she's going to be black and blue before lunch." *Huh? Oh fuck a lame duck.*

"Oh God. I can't believe I did it again. Geez, I'm sorry. But you know, it just sort of feels like I'm falling apart from the inside out. And to tell you the truth, my brother isn't all that much fun to live with and even though I love my sister-in-law, there is only so much she can do to run interference, you know?" Sitting up straighter on Kent's lap as if it would give her a new view of things, Tobi pushed her shoulders back and forced herself to smile. "But…I'll be fine and adversity builds character, right?"

When neither of them said anything for long moments she started to squirm with unease. "Sit still, sweetness, or you're going to derail the conversation we need to have." His words might have sounded rough, but the gleam in his eyes made her suddenly very aware of the fact his cock was rapidly stiffening against her thigh. She managed to hold back her giggle, afraid it might end up sounding hysterical, because right now her world was so out of control she was afraid she was about to be flung into space.

"I'm sorry you've gotten caught up in this, I'd tell you that I'm not usually this much of a train wreck…but, well, I don't want spanked for lying. Remember those old-time carrousels with the horses and zebras and such that were going around and up-and-down at the same time?" When they both nodded she blundered on, "Well I feel like I'm standing in the middle of one of those…where things don't move, but the lights are bright, the music is exceptionally loud, and everything around me is spinning. I can't focus on anything in particular because things are moving too fast for me to zero in on any one problem."

KYLE HAD BEEN frustrated with Tobi's continued attempts to handle things on her own and her willingness to call her brother, who she clearly didn't want to stay with until her description of how overwhelmed she was feeling. Those few words had changed everything, because now he understood that she was simply grasping at straws rather than trying to escape their care. With things falling down around her so quickly, it was no wonder she was struggling. He'd been leaning against the edge of the window while he'd been listening to her, but he pushed away from it, walked closer, and leaned his ass against the edge of Kent's desk. He was close enough he could once again see the dark circles under her eyes. *Christ, they look like fucking bruises they are so dark.* "Kitten, thank you for explaining it so perfectly. I had never considered the implications of everything you've been dealing with and that is really a Cardinal Sin for a Dom and absolutely inexcusable for two of them together."

When she started to speak, he shook his head and placed a finger over her lips. "Hear me out. Let's try to get a little bit more rest because you are exhausted. Then we'll meet with Micah and see what he's got for you and what his investigation is turning up. In the meantime, I'm sure you realize it isn't safe for you to go to work because not only would you be at risk, but you would be endangering your coworkers as well."

Her eyes filled with defeat and tears flooded their pretty green depths. "I know you're right. But I looked for so long before I found this job. And this is a guarantee that I'll be done there. My brother is gonna rip me a new one and I don't even know how things went from sugar to shit so fast....and I really *hate* to cry."

"Well, sweetness, let's get some rest and then we'll tackle each of these problems one at a time. I think you're going to find out that things will work out a lot better than you are expecting." When Kent set her on her feet, Kyle stepped forward, pulled her against his chest, and held her tight for several seconds before leading her down the hall.

When she started to climb up on the bed, Kyle put his hand on her shoulder. "Strip, kitten. No clothes in bed for you...ever. We will always want you naked in our bed." What he didn't add was that if they collared her, she would be naked or nearly so much of the time. And she wouldn't wear anything inside their home unless they specifically allowed it. Kyle watched as she hesitated for just a few seconds and then shrugged out of the shirt and climbed into bed. He wasn't sure if she had really *complied* or if is she was simply too drained to argue the point, but he knew that time would tell.

Chapter Twelve

CHRIS FELDMAN STOOD across the street and watched as a man with sandy blonde hair carried out boxes from Tobi Strobel's charred apartment. The man had spoken with everyone on the scene except him and the irony of that wasn't wasted on Chris. He could hardly believe the bitch had led him on for months and then when he finally got her to go out with him, she acted like she was too fucking good to pay her way. He'd spent a small fortune scoring the tickets to the Snowball gala and hiring a limo, and she still hadn't put out. Most of the women he knew would have been more than happy to "give back a little" for such a sweet ride.

Then she managed to get into the hottest BDSM club in the state just because she had a hissy in front of the owners' mother—hell, the absurdity of *that* still chapped his ass. He didn't know who the asshole was that was currently cleaning out her place, but he was betting he worked for the two rich boys that ran the club. *If she thinks she can fuck those two and then come running back to me when they're done with her without paying the piper, she's in for a big surprise.*

He continued to watch until the guy and the two that had shown up with the boxes had finally seemed satisfied that they had gotten everything and taken off. Following at a safe distance, he watched as they headed west and he was sure they were headed to The Prairie Winds Club until they took an exit and headed south. *Fuck!* He had not been able to make the lanes changes in time to exit and there wasn't another one for three miles. They'd be long gone by the time he got back and now he didn't know for sure where the bitch was.

MICAH HAD KNOWN he was being watched almost from the minute he'd arrived on the scene and part of the reason he'd called Ash and Dex to bring boxes. Dex had snuck out the back door of the piece of shit building Tobi had lived in and scanned the perimeter with a pair of night-vision goggles. The asshole had been so easy to find it had almost been funny. But for him to think they wouldn't notice him following them—well, that was just insulting. They'd lost him easily and then doubled back via back roads to the club.

Ash had helped him box up what was left of Tobi's belongings and there hadn't been much that was worth saving. She had a cedar chest that looked like it contained a few antique quilts and such, and Micah had been pleased to see that those seemed unharmed. The wooden box itself was damaged, but he hoped the club's resident handyman, Don Reynolds, could restore it to a semblance of its former beauty. Micah had learned a long time ago that almost every personal possession could be replaced, but losing something that had sentimental value rather than monetary value was usually the most devastating. And in his opinion, the young woman that had stolen his bosses' hearts had already seen more than her share of heartache.

Micah had done a quick check into Tobi's background

when he'd known she would be interviewing the West brothers. What he'd found had been pathetic, but probably all too common. It certainly was time for this young woman to catch a break. She had only been seven when her mother had died and by all accounts her father had been a mean drunk who was investigated numerous times for child abuse. Teachers and the parents of her friends had turned him in several times over the years, but Tobi had always denied the charges. Officials had noted after each of those interviews that she seemed more afraid of losing her only living parent than she did of his continued abuse.

Tobi's brother was a decade older and had done little to protect his younger sister because he'd left for college a few months after their mother passed and had rarely returned home after that. The brother had become a successful attorney and had evidently called in a lot of favors to keep his father's death in a barroom brawl last year out of the news. Even though Richard Strobel had married well, he still struggled to be accepted into the social circles that he aspired to. Rumors abounded that he was currently considering running for state office.

Tobi, on the other hand, seemed to be well liked by everyone who knew her. Her neighbors had described her as outgoing and genuine. They had been quick to point out that Tobi was the first one to volunteer to help if someone needed a helping hand and that she had often brought groceries to those less fortunate despite the fact she was obviously living well below the poverty line herself.

Breaking in to her employee record at the magazine where she worked hadn't been difficult despite what he was sure the small publishing group believed were adequate safeguards. Her attendance record was nearly perfect and each of her performance reviews had been glowing, but she was still slated to be laid off at the end of the month even though it didn't appear they'd bothered to tell her yet. And now the little subbie had lost most of her possessions at the hands of some jerk. His interview with Tobi's neighbor, Gracie, had given him a name and not surprisingly, it had matched the black SUV sitting just down the street. Dex had found the guy almost immediately and when they'd run his license number and it came back registered to Chris Feldman, Micah hadn't been surprised. His guess was that Feldman was probably trying to get her "down" enough that he could ride in on his white horse and be her knight in shining armor. *Good luck with that, fucker. Even if things don't work out with my bosses, I'll help her stay away from you.*

Micah had asked Ash and Dex to do a perimeter sweep before heading back to their cabin. It had only taken Micah a few minutes to set up some of the tables they kept in the shop for picnics and then spread Tobi's meager possessions out so they could air out. Flipping on the massive overhead exhaust fans, Micah hoped he had managed to salvage enough that she wouldn't feel as though everything she owned had been incinerated. Glancing at his watch, he winced knowing it was going to be a short night. He fired off a text to Don Reynolds about the cedar chest before shutting down the lights and locking up. Micah made his way down the short path to the cabin he used on the weekends and hoped he'd get at least a couple hours of sleep before he met with Kent and Kyle. He didn't like driving into Austin after the club closed because at that time of day it seemed like the streets were filled with crazies. Everyone knew that the percentage of drunks behind the wheel was exponentially higher during the wee hours before dawn and Micah had lost too many friends to that particular brand of stupidity to take any chances.

So much of what he did was internet based or already involved travel that Micah was considering closing his small office in Austin and trying to find a place closer to Prairie Winds. The ranch the elder Wests had just purchased had a large building toward the front of the property, which would be perfect, and he planned to talk to Dean and Dell about that possibility soon. With Jax heading their way next week, it was time to start putting some things together. Stepping into the small cabin, Micah looked at the tiny kitchen and shook his head. Jax McDonald was barely going to fit in the small space and he was going to curse like the sailor he was when he got a look at the kitchen here and at the one in Micah's apartment in town.

Their SEAL team had teased Jax mercilessly about the fact his last name was indelibly linked to fast food, yet he hated it with a unique passion Micah figured was reserved for truly dedicated athletes. While Jax wasn't the gourmet cook that Ash and Dex were, he was still extremely talented and Micah had always been amazed he could make healthy food seem so appealing. Micah was a stereotypical computer nerd, perfectly content to guzzle sludge that had been baking in the coffee maker for the past ten hours and surviving on nothing but greasy burgers with an occasional breakfast eaten out at the local Denny's thrown in for good measure.

At six foot eleven, Jax was so tall his appearance alone was enough to intimidate most people. He was also built like a block of solid brick and mortar. He'd been a power lifter in high school and college and had been one of the few men who hadn't struggled at all with the physical demands of BUDS. Every guy in their class had wanted on

Jax's team because the only thing more impressive than his physical strength was his ability to pull the best from everyone he worked with. The man always looked like he had a suntan and that along with his deep black hair and crystal blue eyes, the guy was a serious chic-magnet.

Micah and Jax had been swim buddies so they had become particularly close. It hadn't taken them long to discover their mutual kinks and to make friends with Kyle and Kent West. When they had eventually learned the West's parents were involved in a poly-relationship, they had barely let Kyle or Kent rest until they'd answered every conceivable question he and Jax had thrown their way. Kyle had finally thrown his hands in the air one night and declared the topic taboo. Then they'd laughed it off and invited Jax and Micah to join them after graduation when they traveled to Texas to spend some time with their family.

Just as Kyle and Kent had promised, their parents were open and straightforward and had patiently answered literally hundreds of questions he and Jax had shot out to them in an almost rapid-fire barrage. Micah didn't think you would probably ever get the West's sons to admit how much they had both also learned during those discussions, but he hadn't missed how attentively the brothers had listened as their parents had explained how difficult it was at times. Micah had found it particularly interesting that none of their challenges had been from the dynamics within the relationship. Every problem they'd encountered had been from the judgments of people outside their inner circle of contacts.

By the time Micah had showered and climbed into bed the sun was just starting to peak over the horizon. As he settled back, he couldn't help but think about the little balls-to-the-wall spitfire he'd met earlier this morning. Gracie Santos was approximately five foot four and her long black hair easily brushed the top of her lush ass. She wasn't stick thin, but had large rounded breasts and an ass that looked like it had been specifically made for paddling. *And with her mouth, she is sure to get plenty of those.* When she'd seen him speaking with the building super, Gracie had crowded in and started rapid-firing questions at him and crowding into his personal space until he'd finally wrapped his large hand around her wrist so she would stop shaking her finger at him. At his touch she had gone instantly silent and dropped her eyes. He'd felt her pulse start to gallop under his fingertips that were softly pressed against her pulse point. When he'd told her to look at him, Micah had watched her eyes go wide and realized the zing of electricity he'd felt when his work-roughened fingers had first brushed over her smooth skin had not been one-sided. The tip of her pink tongue darted out to paint her rose-colored lips and it had taken every bit of the control he had learned as a Dom not to push her against the wall in the small hallway and plunder her mouth.

He had calmly explained to her that Tobi was fine and that he'd be packing up her belongings and taking them to her. When she had volunteered to help, Micah had been grateful for several reasons. First of all, she seemed to be a friend of Tobi's so she was familiar with the lay out of the tiny apartment and knew where to find the most important items quickly. It had also given him a chance to find out about the man Gracie knew had been causing Tobi problems. But most importantly, it had given him a chance to spend more time with her. Each moment had convinced him further that she was very likely the woman he and Jax had dreamed of finding and sharing.

While Gracie had been in Tobi's bathroom packing up her medicine cabinet, Micah had programmed his number into her phone and then quickly dialed it so he'd have her number. He'd pointed out his number to her and asked her to call him if she had any questions or concerns. When he had expressed a concern that Feldman might be a threat to her he'd seen the fear flash in her eyes and had known immediately that she was already afraid of the man who had likely set tonight's blaze. When he asked her if Feldman had already been a problem for her, Micah had seen her eyes darting from side-to-side as if she was afraid the man was watching before she'd quickly nodded.

Laying back and trying to figure out a strategy to introduce Gracie to Jax, Micah found himself lost in the erotic pictures flashing through his mind of her naked flesh pressed in between the two of them. The fantasy became so hot he could barely resist the temptation to take himself in hand and relieve the raging hard-on he'd had since meeting her. Reaching for his phone, Micah typed in two quick messages. The first was to Gracie reminding her to feel free to call him day or night if she had any problems with Feldman. The second to Jax...*I think I've found her.*

Chapter Thirteen

Tobi had spent the entire week dealing with a thousand questions from a hundred different people. Each one of them had asked her if she knew of anyone who might want to hurt her and by Friday she was starting to feel like she should be looking over her shoulder at every turn.

Just as everyone had expected, Tobi had shown up at work on Monday morning and was told she was being laid off due to the economic downturn.

When she'd called Kyle to tell him the news, the only thing he'd said was "Are you okay, kitten?" She knew he had been worried about her when he'd left her off for work and she doubted he'd gone far. *Only because you and Kent prepared me for this and I know I won't be sleeping on the street.* The small guest cottage they'd given her was perfect and they'd assured her it was hers for as long as she needed it.

Taking a deep breath, Tobi answered, "Yes…well, I will be as soon as I get out of here." Chris Feldman had been in a meeting when she arrived at Austin Gardens and Homes, but he'd been standing in the hallway as she'd carried out the small box of personal items she'd cleared out of her desk. As she'd made her way down the hallway to the elevators that would take her to the exit, she had to pass by his office and he'd made sure he was leaning against the doorframe. Leaning probably wasn't a very good description considering the man was almost as round as he was tall and his body completely filled the doorway.

"Gosh, do I smell smoke?" His leering and menacing laugh sent a chill up Tobi's spine.

"I doubt it, I haven't even been back to my apartment. But it's very interesting you would know about that when I didn't tell anyone here at work. I'll make sure to share that with the investigators I'm speaking with later today." Tobi knew she shouldn't provoke him, but he was such an ass that it was difficult to resist.

"Be careful, Tobi. That was an awful accident and I'd hate to see anything happen to that hot little number that lives across the hall from you. On the other hand—where is she moving when that rat hole you lived in closes later this month? Maybe she'd like to hear about my *rent to own* plan." His thinly veiled threat against Gracie terrified Tobi, because she wasn't sure Gracie would be able to control her temper enough to walk away from a fight with the man she already despised. Gracie was fiercely loyal and she hated Chris because of the hell he'd put Tobi through, evidently he figured out how close they were.

Tobi worked hard to school her expression and simply kept walking without responding to his comment. Kyle had picked her up less than five minutes later. He'd walked into the lobby as if he'd owned the place, set the box she'd been carrying on the floor, and then pulled her into his arms. Tobi hadn't realized how tightly she was wound until she'd felt his strength surround her and that was when the tears started to fall. She cried silently for several minutes and he simply held her until the storm had passed.

Kyle always smelled like fresh air and sunshine along with a hint of cologne that was like a whispered promise of wicked nights, and just breathing him in calmed her. When she finally pulled back a bit, he kissed her forehead. "Come on, kitten. Let's go before I strip you and fuck you right here. Even though I know we'd both feel better, I'm pretty sure the lady at the reception desk wouldn't be impressed."

Tobi giggled, "Irene? Are you kidding? She'd have a video posted to You Tube by the time we pulled out of the parking lot." Waving to the elderly woman who'd been one of the few people in the building who had befriended her, she let Kyle lead her from the building.

After he'd settled her in his truck and fastened her safety belt, Kyle had brushed a kiss over her lips, "That place is now history, kitten. I don't want you worrying about that job anymore, do you understand? I want you to put it out of your mind and focus on your future, because that is where Kent and I are." His words had been the perfect end to a job she hadn't ever been that fond of anyway so she simply nodded her head in agreement.

Either Kyle or Kent had accompanied her to every appointment she'd had during the rest of the week concerning the fire. She'd talked to so many detectives their faces were starting to blur together and none of them had appeared terribly interested in helping her until Kent had pulled one of the more blatantly disinterested men out into the hall. The man had sulked down the hall and returned with a tall blond man with deep blue eyes. He smiled warmly at Kent as he approached and it was obvious the two men knew each other.

When Kent stepped back in the small glass enclosed office she'd been waiting in, he'd introduced her, saying "Sweetness, I'd like you to meet Captain Parker Andrews." Kent hadn't told her that Captain Andrews was a member of the club, but the instant he'd turned toward her Tobi had known he was a Dom and dropped her eyes. She'd been surprised to see his outstretched hand come into her view and she'd blinked at it for several seconds. Kent had leaned down and whispered against her ear, "Good call, sweetness. Yes, Master Parker, as he is known at the club, is a Dom. But right now, he's the *last* person you are going to have to tell your story to in the police department."

When she slowly reached out and placed her hand in his, Captain Andrews smiled and shook her hand. "It's nice to meet you, Tobi. I hear you have been getting the runaround and I'm here to put an end to that." True to his word he'd listened carefully, ask her questions no one else had thought of and then thanked her politely for her patience. By the time they'd left the police precinct, Tobi's body was finally caving in to the exhaustion she'd been battling all week. She stumbled on the front steps and if Kent hadn't already had his arm around her, she was certain she would have tumbled to the bottom of the concrete steps.

"Love, you are supposed to ask for help when you need it. I'm fairly certain my brother and I have mentioned that a time or two over the past week. But apparently words aren't penetrating that rapid fire mind of yours, so I think we'll see if we can't find another way to reinforce the lesson this evening." His threat of punishment didn't frighten her and she was certain he knew that it actually upped her arousal level by several degrees. Kent had helped her to his truck and secured her safety belt before carefully reclining her seat. "I want you to rest on the way home." He must have seen the argument in her eyes because he quickly silenced her with a kiss. "Love, there are dark circles under your eyes again and you've lost weight this week. What you need to learn right now is that my brother and I will not stand idly by and watch you put yourself in danger, either physically or emotionally. And before you get all cranky, consider this—we would step in to help any of our friends, not as quickly or with the same *solutions,* but we'd certainly both be *heard,* I promise you." Tobi wanted to argue with him, but she knew he was right and she just didn't have the energy in that moment to fight a losing battle so she had just nodded and closed her eyes.

KENT WATCHED AS Tobi's eyelids fluttered once and then her long lashes brushed over but didn't hide the dark purple under her eyes. He and Kyle had watched her closely all week hoping she would rein herself in and begin taking care of herself. But she had continued to simply push to the point she'd nearly collapsed on the front steps of the police station. She'd been sound asleep by the time he'd rounded the truck, opened the driver's door, and had barely stirred during the entire drive home.

He knew that she hadn't called her brother yet and he wondered how long she thought she could delay the confrontation. Kent didn't doubt the lawyer with obvious social and political ambitions was going to be none too pleased to find out his younger sister was working for a kink club and living on the grounds. And when he got wind that she was involved with not one, but both of the club's owners, Kent suspected the man was probably going to blow a gasket. They had already prepared for Richard Strobel's reaction. They'd asked Micah to find out if the man didn't have an Achilles heel or two they'd be able to use to "persuade" him to back off any judgment he'd think to express about his sister.

They had discussed a preemptive strike, but had decided they didn't want to betray Tobi's fragile trust by going behind her back to confront her brother. In Kent's opinion, the asshole deserved any and all fallout he might get just because he'd left his sister to live in virtual squalor for the past two years. Despite Micah's report about the building being a disaster, he'd been impressed that Tobi's apartment had appeared organized. Even stating she seemed to be the type to keep a clean apartment because if there was organization, there was cleanliness, even if the looks of it after the fire, most would be hard pressed to tell it. Kent smiled to himself as he made his way down the highway because Micah Drake was meticulously clean and organized, so his observation about Tobi's apartment had been one hell of a compliment.

When Kent had carried her into the elevator she'd shifted in his arms and he'd looked down into clear green eyes that seemed to be trying to bring their surroundings into focus. "Go back to sleep, sweetness. I'm going to put you to bed here because I need to get downstairs for a meeting and I want to be sure you rest a bit more. Kyle will be up in a few minutes to check on you, so you'd better be sleeping when he gets here." Kent made his way off the elevator and into the bedroom before he thought she had even brought him into focus when he sat her on her feet.

She'd swayed on her feet as he had stripped her, but she'd managed to crawl on to the bed and give him a great view of her newly waxed pussy. He was glad they had made her take the time out for a half day of pampering at two different spas Regi had recommended. They had needed to keep her busy for the day, but it was more about their plans for various ways they were going to enjoy all that sensitive bare skin. Walking away from the bed had been torture and he hoped like hell that his raging hard-on was manageable by the time he made it to the back of the club. He needed to meet with contractors to review plans for the addition they wanted built because they had set a very aggressive timeline for the project. Once they'd finalized the basic plans, they'd be consulting Tobi and Regi both for specifics of the design.

Clint, from E.G.A. Fabrication, had already agreed to do the outside metalwork and interior displays. When Kent had called Clint, they had brainstormed various ideas and he and Kyle were both anxious to see what their friend came up with. The guy was a master craftsman with a wicked sense of humor and firsthand knowledge of the lifestyle so they didn't doubt his designs would quickly become the focal point in each of the small shops.

Kent stopped by the office and found Kyle surrounded by reports. "Don't forget to go up and check on Tobi in a few minutes. She finally pushed herself over the edge and nearly collapsed on the steps at the police department." At Kyle's startled look, Kent nodded. "It was a good thing I had my hand on her already or I wouldn't have caught her. She was sleeping when I left upstairs, but I don't know how long she'll sleep unless one of us is there."

Kyle had leaned back in his enormous leather office chair and seemed to be considering Kent's words. "I wonder how long until she realizes how much better she rests when at least one of us is with her?" They had attributed the fact that she didn't sleep well when she was alone to the dangerous neighborhood she'd lived in and that the walls of her apartment were little more than sturdy cardboard. He and Kyle had both visited the site with Micah earlier in the week while Tobi had been at the spas. They had asked her to evaluate both facilities and their services in hopes they'd find one to offer a spot in the new forum shops. She'd enjoyed her time at both locations and had given them incredibly detailed information about both organizations. And while she'd been buffed and waxed, they had gotten the chance to do a bit of fact-finding of their own.

Chapter Fourteen

Tobi remembered Kent carrying her into the elevator and then mentioning Kyle, but everything else was fuzzy. As she lay back trying to sort it through in her mind she suddenly realized she wasn't alone. "You are thinking awfully hard, kitten. Care to share?" Letting her gaze sweep over the eye candy that was Kyle West was no hardship...no hardship at all. Good Lord just looking at him sent a wave of cream into her core. When she fidgeted and twisted in the bed, he raised a brow as the corners of his mouth turned up ever so slightly. "Problem, kitten? And you still need to answer both questions, babe."

In Tobi's mind Kyle's voice was like the soft leather strips of the flogger they'd shown her when she'd toured the theme rooms downstairs. His words sent blood racing through her body and sensitized every single inch. He'd used the same voice during her tour and it had felt like she could lose herself in his words alone. Each of the rooms had been decorated in various themes but none were garish, and that had actually surprised her. All of the research she'd done had shown rooms that seemed so cheesy she'd actually caught herself looking for velvet pictures of Elvis or those damned poker playing dogs.

Coming back to the present, Tobi looked up at Kyle and blinked several times trying to remember what he'd asked her. "Oh, sorry. I was just trying to find all of the pieces of the puzzle so I can figure out how I got here. And then…well, your…umm, well your voice made me think about something else and you know how it is. Before I knew it my mind was chasing the shiny bunny through the trees and then that damned kangaroo hopped across the path and…"

Kyle's barked laugh finally ended her rambling, "Kitten, I do believe I understand what you are saying. And you are one of the brightest women I know, but you are off-the-chart ADD. Were you ever tested for that when you were a kid?"

His question surprised her more because it was so insightful than intrusive. "Yeah, but my parents weren't really very good at following through with anything like medications, so I just had to learn ways to cope. I was lucky, because I had a couple of teachers who had the same problem and they helped me figure out ways to be functional…well, at least most of the time." She could feel her face heating and when she looked down she realized the sheet she'd thought was covering her bare breasts was actually being twisted in her nervous fingers and her tightly peaked nipples were practically screaming for attention.

"Well, we'll talk more about that some other time. Right now I want to know if you are still tired or if you are hungry. We have big plans for you tonight and you're going to need the energy, kitten." He was moving toward the bed with a grace that spoke of years of Special Forces training and working in places where stealth often meant the difference between life and death. His casual grace reminded her of a jungle cat on the prowl and suddenly she felt like prey waiting to be devoured.

Tobi had been so caught up in watching him move that she didn't answer until his fingers lifted her chin so her eyes met his. "I'm not really tired, but I am hungry. Let me grab my clothes and then I'll head down to my—" she cut off her sentence at Kyle's narrowed eyes. "What?"

"Kitten, sometimes I swear you are deliberately obtuse because I know there is no way a woman as bright as you are could not understand this. I did not come up here to send you on your way. I came up to make sure you were resting. Since you aren't, I'm going to fix you something to eat while you take a shower." He'd pulled her gently from the bed and all the time he'd been speaking he'd been ushering her into the bathroom. Kyle started water and then when he was satisfied the water was just right kissed her on the forehead before turning her and giving her bare ass a smack causing her to shriek and step under the spray. He chuckled, "Hurry up, kitten. I have a surprise for you so come out to the kitchen after you are finished in here."

Tobi was sure she'd set some sort of speed record showering, but then just as she was ready to step out of the bathroom she stopped to consider what the surprise might be and hesitated. On one hand she was starving, but on the other…well, Kent and Kyle's surprises tended to be a bit over the top. She'd been standing staring at the closed door when she heard a soft chuckle behind her. Spinning around, she gasped at the sight of Kent standing with his legs shoulder width apart and a pair of well-worn Levis riding low on his slender hips. The black T-shirt he was wearing molded him like a second skin and highlighted every bump and ridge of his muscular torso. His hair was wet and his feet bare so Tobi assumed he'd just come from his own shower. God but he was amazing. It was moments like this that she wanted to run her hands over every inch of both men. He cocked his brow at her and smiled. "Like what you see, love?" She nodded because she was still taking in the delicious sight in front of her and wasn't anxious to give it up just yet. "Sweetness, that door isn't going to open itself. Did Kyle scare you with the promise of a surprise?"

Placing his hand on her elbow he began walking her down the hallway after he had finally opened the door. "Yes, a little bit. You know most men surprise women with flowers or a basket from Bed & Bath, right? But you guys seem to shop in a whole different venue. And now I'm working for you to set up a Pervs-R-Us emporium." Just thinking about what they might have dreamed up for her was making her pussy wet and she could already feel the need pulsing through her. Her nipples were so tight they were almost painful and she could feel the flush working its way up her neck and by the time they reached the kitchen her cheeks were on fire because they were practically burning.

KENT HAD MADE his way back upstairs just as Kyle had come into the kitchen. They'd talked briefly about the security breach that Micah had noted during the afternoon and their concerns about the evening they'd planned being disrupted. They'd also reviewed their plans for Tobi's first night as a club member. Her finished paperwork was spread out on the table. As expected her medical lab work had cleared easily and they'd also placed their own out for her to look over. Kent couldn't help but grin when he remembered Tobi's surprise when they'd taken her in the back door of Kirk Evans's medical office. Kirk had agreed to do the lab work as a rush order if they would introduce him and his medical practice partner, Brian Bennett, to

Regi. Because they were members of the club, he and Kyle had known Kirk and Brian were both Doms, but they hadn't known the pair was looking for a full-time submissive. Both men were well known in the BDSM community for their firm hands when it came to dealing with subs, but they were also totally committed to the safe, sane, and consensual tenant that was the Golden Rule at The Prairie Winds Club, so he and Kyle had agreed to introduce them to Regi this weekend.

Kirk and Brian didn't come out to the club as often as they wanted to because they had been busy rebuilding their practices after moving to the edge of the city. After their office had been broken into and robbed the third time in less than a year, the two physicians had decided to move to a safer location. They seemed to enjoy the slower pace of a smaller practice and they'd laughed about their "commute" because they'd actually built their office onto the end of the sprawling home they'd purchased fifteen minutes east of Prairie Winds.

The two doctors had been friends for years and from what Kent could tell, their biggest difference was in their looks. Kirk was six foot two with black hair and dark eyes. His dark skin and muscular build hinted at his Native American heritage. Brian was taller, standing six foot four with shaggy shoulder length blonde hair and sparkling blue eyes. Kent and Kyle had known both men since high school and Brian had always seemed out of place in western Texas. They'd teased him for years that he and Micah were both misplaced California surfers. Both men had become physicians and then specialized in the care of women after Brian's older sister died while giving birth.

Tobi had been mortified that both he and Kyle had stayed in the room during her exam, but the good doctor had patiently explained that it was actually quite common with his patients who were a part of the BDSM community. Kent knew they wouldn't be able to fuck Tobi without condoms in the club itself because that was a rule no one was allowed to overlook, but they sure were looking forward to it in private. They had a strict zero-tolerance clause in the membership agreement—one violation and your membership was immediately terminated and you were not eligible to re-apply for two years.

The sound of thunder in the distance caught Kent's attention and brought him back to his conversation with Kyle. "Have you asked Regi to keep tabs on the weather?" They'd gotten into the habit of having Regi or Tank mention the forecast to members as they entered the club so no one could claim they'd been caught unaware.

"Yes, she'll be posting the information and drawing it to the attention of all members and their guests as they enter. I'm almost finished here. Why don't you go see what is taking Tobi so long. My guess is that I spooked her when I mentioned I had a surprise for her. And since I'm sure she isn't expecting paperwork, I'm going to see what I can snag out of the playroom—don't want to disappoint her you know."

Kent was already making his way down the hall and shaking his head at his brother's antics when he decided to check on Tobi using the back door into the master suite's bath. The door was well hidden and they'd built it as a secondary fire and security exit. Each room in their home had at least two possible exits. Their years of military service had taught them well and they never wanted to feel cornered in their own home. When he'd opened the door Tobi had been standing with nothing on but the steel gray towel she'd wrapped around her small torso as she stared at the closed door in front of her. He stayed still and watched her reflection in the mirror as she bit her lower lip and debated quietly with herself about what the surprise might be.

Mentally shaking his head at her worried expression, he finally let her know he was there and he let the laugh he'd been holding back bubble up his chest. Her eyes had given away how startled she'd been to find him standing behind her but then her gaze had moved down and then back up his body like a sensual caress and he'd almost shuddered at the heat he'd seen flaming in her eyes. For the first time, he understood what subs meant when they said they could feel a Dom's look almost like a touch, because he'd been able to feel Tobi's appreciation that was for sure. He'd asked her if she liked what she saw thinking it would snap her out of it, but she'd merely nodded as her pupils had dilated even further.

Laughing, he'd moved past her to open the door and then taken her elbow and started down the hall. When he'd asked if she was nervous about the surprise he'd felt her shudder. Just as they reached the edge of the kitchen he'd turned to her, "Give me the towel, love." Kent had to hold back his laughter because he really did love the way she stood in front of him and blinked as if she was confused by the instruction. "Tobi." Kent had let his Dom voice through and she'd reacted immediately handing him the towel. "Beautiful. Now, let's see what Kyle has made for you to eat." Tobi's skin was flushed beautifully with her arousal and he could smell her sweet cream over the citrus scent of her body wash. Her skin practically glowed and her bare pussy lips already glistened with her arousal.

Kyle was leaning against the counter with his arms crossed over his chest and one ankle crossed over the other watching for them. He smiled when they walked around the corner. "Kitten, you look lovely." Kent gave him a silent hand signal for *afraid* and saw his brother's almost imperceptible nod of acknowledgement. Their Special Forces trainers hadn't been surprised at how quickly the two of them had picked up on hand-sign communication. They had explained that twins often picked up the technique quicker than most soldiers simply because they had usually been using similar methods for years—whether consciously or not. As sexual Dominants they'd found the ability to communicate silently invaluable and used it often, but they would have to be particularly cautious with Tobi. The bright young woman standing naked in front of him wouldn't be fooled if she even caught a glimpse of a signal. He pulled her back against his chest and stroked his hands up and down her arms, smiling to himself as he remembered how effective it had been when they'd blindfolded her. They'd known it would enhance her other senses and they had hoped it would help her focus on what she was feeling as well. Now they would need to use it to protect their "chatter" from being visible in one of the hundreds of mirrors positioned around the club so they would likely be using blindfolds often.

"Come here, kitten." Kyle's words hadn't been loud, but Kent grinned when he felt the small shudder that moved through Tobi's muscles. He stepped back and pressed his hand possessively at the base of her spine to gently guide her to his brother. They had noticed over the past week that Tobi appeared to respond really well to that particular touch and she seemed to unconsciously time her movements so his or Kyle's hand was in constant contact with her. Her subconscious efforts to find comfort in their touch was a clear indicator of the depth of her submissive nature.

After Kyle had wrapped his arms around her, Kent

watched as his brother kissed the top of her head. "I can't tell you how much I love watching you walk naked into the room, kitten. Your body tells both my brother and I exactly what you need and we intend to meet each and every one of those needs tonight." Kyle smoothed his hands up and down Tobi's slender back several times before cupping her ass. "Before we eat I've got a few toys that I want to introduce you to." When Kyle moved to the side Kent saw a folded towel at the edge of the counter and grinned at his brother as Kyle leaned her over the counter so her stomach was on the towel, but her bare breasts were pressing against the cool granite countertop. They both chuckled when she gasped at the cold against her already pebbled nipples and Kyle gave her a quick swat when her reflexes kicked in and she tried to stand back up. "Stay put. Spread your legs and lift your ass as you arch your back." When she didn't immediately comply, Kyle gave her two more swats on each of her ass cheeks. "Right now, Tobi, or I'll take you over my knee and paddle you until I think you have learned your lesson. And then we'll make sure you spend the entire evening at the club nicely displaying your lovely red ass cheeks from the stockade."

Kent stepped forward and ran his fingers through the soaking folds of her sex. "Well, brother, I do believe that wasn't quite the threat you might have intended it to be." They both laughed as Tobi tried to push back against his fingers, moaning softly. Kent pulled his fingers away and swatted each of her pink cheeks. "You're getting ahead of yourself, sweetness." He moved to the other side of the small counter and secured her wrists above her head and kept them clasped in his large hand. "Now hold very still and accept the gifts we've got for you. Oh and don't come, love."

Chapter Fifteen

KYLE WATCHED TOBI'S reaction to Kent's admonishment that she wasn't allowed to come and had to hide his smile when she gave Kent a look that was easy to interpret. Evidently Kent thought so too because he nodded to Kyle, clearly wanting him to give her a couple of swats for the glare. Kyle didn't hold back and made sure she'd be able to tell the difference between a punishment spanking and the erotic spanks they'd given her a couple of times during the week. "What the fuck? That hurt, why'd you hit me?" When she started to stand up Kyle leaned over her shoulder and bit down just enough for her to realize she was being held in place.

"Those were punishment swats, kitten. They were supposed to hurt. And I did not *hit* you, I spanked you for glaring at one of your Masters. Do you want to use your safe word, Tobi?" Kyle had taken his time with his response so the heat from her swats had enough time to begin the magical morphing from pain to arousal that he knew she was going to experience. He palmed her ass cheeks, massaging them gently before sliding his fingers through the soaking wet folds of her labia. "Kitten, you are soaking wet. Do you still want to tell me how much you hated those swats? Or have you already noticed that your body has begun to blur that line between pain and pleasure?" Pushing two fingers deep inside her, Kyle smiled at the way she lifted her ass in invitation and moaned. "Kitten, you are going to earn more swats if I don't get answers to my questions."

"No. No. Yes."

He and Kent both chuckled at her. "Very good, kitten. Although I would have preferred complete answers, you did actually answer each question, so we're good to go. Now, we have something special picked out for you to wear tonight and even though it's lovely it still needs a bit of embellishment." Sliding open the cabinet door where he'd hidden the toys, Kyle pulled out a medium sized butt plug and rolled it in a small dish of lube he'd already prepared. They had introduced Tobi to butt plugs earlier in the week, but this time she'd be wearing a larger one and she would be keeping it in long enough to stretch her enough she'd be able to take them both later tonight. Fucking her slowly with the plug, he reached around her and started circling his fingers around her swollen clit and grinned when he saw Kent unzipping his pants.

"Take me into your mouth, sweetness." Kyle watched as Tobi opened her mouth wide and almost threw herself forward so Kent's cock had probably hit the back of her throat.

"Jesus fucking Christ. Oh baby, your mouth is unbelievable." Kent's voice sounded like sand paper and Kyle knew he wouldn't be able to hang on long so he quickly slid the egg vibrator into her wet channel as he continued pressing the plug into her rear hole. The small remote was in Kent's reach and subtly, he slid his hand over it and nodded.

Kyle pinched Tobi's clit, bit down on the lobe of her ear, and commanded her to, "Come for us, kitten." Just before he'd spoken he'd felt both toys begin pulsing and her entire body jerked before stiffening and then she seemed to be coming apart at the seams as she pulled back marginally from Kent and her scream echoed around the kitchen. The vibration of her scream was a sweet torture if Kent's pained expression was anything to go by. Kyle smiled to himself because his imagination was running rampant, and just thinking about Tobi's hot mouth surrounding his cock was almost enough to have him losing his own control. Kyle could feel Tobi's sweet cream coating his fingers and he lightened his touch on her now sensitive sex and wondered if she even realized he'd already pushed the larger plug in place. He carefully removed his fingers because he certainly didn't want her too sore to enjoy the rest of the other activities they had planned for her this evening.

Kent seemed to be holding back until he knew Tobi was once again focused and in the moment. "Sweetness, I'm barely holding on and once I start fucking this sweet mouth again, I'm going to come very quickly. Are you ready to swallow every drop I give you?" Kyle knew Kent's voice was rough just from the effort it was taking him to hold back, but his fingers were slowly caressing the sides of Tobi's flushed cheeks.

Once she'd regained her focus her grin was almost daring, "Oh yeah" was all she'd managed to say before Kent had set a quick pace of thrusts—some fast and shallow, others slow and deeper. The random pattern was Kent's attempt to keep Tobi on edge until he was ready for her to come again. Kyle reached for the remote control for the device Kent slid down her back as he caressed her spine. Almost immediately, Kent leaned his head back and moaned as he finally surrendered to the satisfaction he'd been holding back. Kyle had intended to turn on both devices and send her over a few seconds later, but before he could he watched in wonder as her body responded with its own orgasm while she was hungrily swallowing Kent's cum. *Well, kitten, you just played into our hands perfectly.*

TOBI KNEW WHEN Kent's seed first pulsed over her tongue that the erotic taste of him and the feel of it hitting the back of her throat was going to make her come a second time without permission but there wasn't a thing she could do to stop it. She felt like she had been launched into space as the bright spots of light flickered behind her eyelids. Floating in the bliss of the moment, she relaxed her jaw muscles and let Kent's still partially erect cock push in all the way so she could swallow around him and massage him with her throat muscles. As Kent slowly pulled away she relished the feeling of power that washed over her as she thought about how she pushed his control to the very edge before he'd grabbed her and pulled her headfirst into the canyon of sexual oblivion with him.

But her self-congratulations were short-lived when Kyle leaned over and spoke against her ear. The feeling of his hot tongue licking over the sensitive skin behind her ear caused goose bumps to race over her sweat dampened skin. "Kitten? If I'm not mistaken, you just climaxed without permission." Tobi might not be functioning with all cylinders working at capacity just yet, but she sure knew an opportunity to keep quiet when she hit one front and center. Since he technically hadn't asked her anything she didn't answer him, but she couldn't help the shiver of response that her traitorous body let fly. And she damned her fair complexion as well when she felt her cheeks flushing and knew they must be bright red.

"Sweetness, I hope like hell you don't play poker." Kent's chuckle had her looking up and her body seemed to follow as she started to stand. A couple of quick swats to her bare ass reminded her that she was still supposed to be bent over the counter. "We're going to deal with your punishment a little later on this evening love. But right now, you just hold on while my brother cleans you up a bit so we can have some dinner.

"But...um, the plug..." she knew her words had trailed off and she hated how needy they had sounded even to her own ears.

Kyle leaned down and bit first one and then the other ass cheek, reminding her how sensitive they were after her swats. The warm cloth he was using to clean her was soft and before she'd really processed how embarrassing it was to have a man who looked like a sex God cleaning her soaked sex he was already patting her dry. "Trust me, kitten. We are fully aware that you still have our surprises inside your sweet body. That is exactly where they will stay until one of us removes them, do you understand?"

"Yes, I understand. Sir." She'd hastily added the last word and let out a deep breath when Kyle smiled and nodded.

"Good, girl. Don't worry, you'll get used to the protocol before you know it. You're doing really well by the way." Tobi wasn't sure why his simple words of praise meant so much, but she felt her inner child doing a little happy dance and gave herself a mental high-five for good measure. She had been working all week reminding herself that she was just an employee and they were merely training her, even though she knew it was a useless attempt to prevent her heart from getting involved. She knew getting her hopes up about a long-term relationship with them was a slippery slope to disaster, but she could already feel herself sliding headfirst toward a broken heart.

Tobi had learned a long time ago that the "haves" and the "have nots" rarely intermingled for more than a one night stand. She considered her brother's marriage to be one of the rare exceptions to that rule and had always credited his incredible intelligence and college education for his success. Tobi wasn't jealous of her brother. She was actually quite proud of all he'd overcome and all he had achieved. And she loved him as only a sister could, but that didn't mean that she liked him very much, because quite frankly he was an arrogant ass.

Chapter Sixteen

KYLE HAD BEEN looking out over the club's members as they enjoyed their various activities, but his mind couldn't seem to let go of the words Tobi had been speaking about her brother before they'd sat down to eat. He smiled to himself when he remembered the startled look on Tobi's face when her warm skin had connected with the chair. Kyle wasn't sure what had been the bigger surprise for her, the cool leather or the butt plug that would have pressed against very sensitive tissues when she'd sat down. Her gasp and whispered curses had caused he and Kent to both laugh out loud.

Micah stepped up beside him and looked at him with a brow raised in question. "Problem?" Kyle appreciated the succinct communication style they shared as former teammates and that in turn reminded him that he and Kent planned to take Tobi with them next week when they met with Clint about the metalwork designs for the addition. Tobi had some great ideas and they were anxious to introduce the two of them. Clint's family had invited them to stay for dinner and they knew Tobi and Kimberly would hit it off as well. *Jesus, Joseph, and Mary. I think her subject hopping must be contagious.*

Kyle shook his head at his own distraction before answering. "Not really, there is just something about the whole situation with Tobi's brother that is setting off all my internal alarms. I don't really have a reason to believe he might be a threat to Tobi, even though I think he's a selfish dick."

They stood watching as Kent danced with Tobi for several minutes before Micah responded. "Don't discount your gut feelings. I agree that any guy with his political aspirations who has that many skeletons in his closet is a train wreck looking for a place to happen. Hell, the guy has had every opportunity in the world to be a legitimate success, but he's aligned himself with some pretty nasty people including his in-laws."

Kyle looked on as Tobi tugged on the hem of the obscenely short dress they'd chosen for her to wear. The crystals on the butt plug were catching the light and drawing everyone's attention to her lush curves and for a minute Kyle questioned their decision to begin introducing their sweet sub to the joys of exhibitionism. Kent grabbed her hand and gave her ass a good swat before settling his palm on her lower back so the dress rode up and his handprint was clearly visible above the sparkly plug. Kyle and Micah both chuckled.

"She really is lovely, Kyle. And it's easy to see how happy she is making the two of you. I hope it works out for you all." Kyle caught the wistful tone in Micah's voice and nodded his thanks. Just as he turned to ask his friend if he'd heard from Tobi's friend, Gracie, Micah's phone beeped with an incoming message. Kyle looked down and saw Gracie's name on the screen but couldn't read the message. Micah's growled, "Son of a fucking bitch" had Kyle turning to face him.

"What's wrong?"

Micah didn't answer because he was already dialing. "Gracie? Where are you darlin'?" Kyle could hear her excited tone, but couldn't understand the words. "Baby, slow down and tell me what direction you are traveling and what you see right now. Okay you are about ten miles from the front gate. We'll be out there waiting. Slow down just enough to make the corner and then keep driving until you get to the club. Pull right up to the front door and I'll have someone there waiting for you." Kyle heard her chattering again before Micah added, "No, don't stop at the gate, just keep going. Now nail it, baby."

Before Micah had even finished speaking Kyle had signaled Kent to come over. He was already on the phone putting every one the club's employees on alert before Kent made it to his side. Kyle had made sure the guys in the gatehouse knew what was headed their way and quickly explained what little he knew about the situation to Kent and Tobi. When Tobi turned and started running to the front door, Kent had cursed and taken off after her. Kyle had to laugh at Tobi's shriek of surprise when Kent scooped her up after taking less than a half dozen steps. "Damn it to Hades, put me down you big lug. Boy, I really fracking hate being portable. Put me down, Kent, I've got to get to Gracie. She never asks for help so something has to be horribly wrong." Kyle walked alongside Kent as they quickly made their way through the crowded club.

Kent's voice broke no argument when he finally spoke, "Tobi. *Stop*. You are already in a peck of trouble, love, so I suggest you stop talking. I'd like you to stop and consider that there are several former Special Forces soldiers on our security team." At that moment they walked into the reception area just as the front door opened.

"And another one just walked in the door." Kyle couldn't keep the smile from his face as they came face to face with Jax McDonald. "Glad to see you, brother. Drop your bag over there and Tank will take care of it. Let's go." Jax didn't miss a beat. Dropping his bag, he turned and followed Kyle.

"What's up? I met several cars racing toward the road and the front gate was open and the guys up there just waved me through like they wanted me out of the way." Kyle knew he and Kent were both tall, but at six foot eleven inches, Jax dwarfed everyone around him. The man would probably be intimidating as hell if it weren't for the southern boy charm he could turn on and off like it was connected to a switch. His black hair was longer than Kyle had ever seen it, letting him know his friend had probably been working off-grid for a while.

"Has Micah mentioned a woman named Gracie to you?" Kyle tried to keep his voice lowered so Tobi wouldn't hear, but considering the quick look she'd given him, he knew he hadn't been successful.

"Yes, on several occasions as a matter of fact." Kyle could hear the amusement in his voice and had to smile.

"Well, she is incoming. Status unknown, but Micah cleared a path for her and she should be—" he stopped speaking just as they heard the sound of a car—or at least he assumed the high pitched whining mechanical racket coming up the drive was a car. *Christ, how on earth did she make it this far in that wreck?*

Obviously Kent hadn't kept a good hold on Tobi because she was moving across the open concrete in front of the stairway before the car had even made the turn to park in front of the club. All three men lunged for her, but Jax's long stride and arms reached her first, and he plucked her up just as the tiny car rocked to a stop exactly where Tobi had been standing.

Kyle and Kent both growled at her behavior and Jax

laughed, "Oh, little sub, you are in it deep. Hope you can swim, sweet cheeks." Jax turned and handed Tobi off to Kyle before returning his attention to the woman in the car.

Kyle tightened his hold on Tobi when Jax opened the door and a battered young Latino woman fell into his arms. Kyle heard Jax's softly muttered curses as he scooped Gracie into his arms. "*Cariño*. Careful. Let's get you inside where we can check you out, okay?"

Gracie's eyes widened as Jax started to scoop her up into his arms. Kyle knew Jax hadn't missed the look of panic in her eyes and he stopped moving immediately. Without ever taking his eyes off Gracie, he addressed Tobi. "Sweet cheeks, my name is Jax McDonald. I am friends with both of your Masters and Micah. Please assure Gracie that I would never hurt her."

Kyle felt Tobi go lax in his hold as she let out the breath she'd been holding. Both he and Kent had told her that Jax would be arriving. They had also mentioned the fact that Jax and Micah had been looking for a sub to share since deciding to retire from the teams. "Gracie, it is okay honey. I know he's a big guy, but he's a friend of Micah's and...well, the men I've been telling you about. Please, let us get you into the club." Kyle watched as Gracie dropped her gaze and nodded. Jax didn't waste any time repositioning her so he could slide his arms gently around her shoulders and under her knees. He took the wide steps two at a time as he quickly made his way inside.

JAX HAD FELT a red-hot rage boil inside his chest at his first sight of Gracie Santos. The bruises on her slender neck were clearly made by someone who had been trying to choke her. He was worried about the swelling that had probably already started restricting her ability to speak and swallow since she had simply nodded rather than spoken her answer to Tobi. All Special Forces soldiers had medic training and Jax had seen a woman in Kazakhstan die after her airway swelled closed several hours after her husband tried to choke her before he'd left her along the side of the road.

Jax hadn't wanted to set Gracie down on the exam table when they'd reached the club's first aid station so he'd just held her until Kyle led in a physician dressed in leathers. Obviously the man was a member of the club and had already been on-site. Jax had heard so much about Gracie from Micah that he felt as if he knew her already, but he reminded himself that didn't mean she knew him.

Kyle introduced him to Brian Bennett, and explained that the Dom was also a local physician specializing in the care of women. When Jax had settled her on the table and started to step back Gracie had grasped several of his fingers and held tight. He stood alongside the table and leaned over to brush a soft kiss over her scraped forehead. *"Cariño?* Do you want me to stay with you?" His heart soared at her quick nod, but her moan of pain at the sharp movement made his heart clench.

The doctor smiled at him and nodded his approval before he started speaking softly to Gracie. It was obvious she wasn't able to speak but he noticed she kept making movements with her free hand and he picked up her fingers and kissed them. *"Cariño,* are you signing?"

Tobi stepped forward quickly and smiled. "Gracie works with deaf Spanish speaking children as a volunteer. She understands their difficulty reading lips when they don't know English because her younger brother had the same problem when their family first moved to the U.S. when they were young kids." Tobi looked up at Jax, "Do you sign? Because Gracie has tried to teach me, but I'm really miserable at it." Jax saw the fire in Gracie's eyes as she shook her head back and forth before wincing. Tobi giggled, "Don't get snarky with me, my friend. You know I suck at signing."

Jax nodded, "As a matter of fact I do sign and for a similar reason. I learned when my sister lost her hearing after she had meningitis." He kissed Gracie's slender fingers again before nodding to the doctor. "Go ahead, doc. You ask and I'll relay Gracie's answers for you." Just as he spoke the words Micah burst into the room. His friend took in the room in a heartbeat noting Jax's proximity to Gracie and Jax saw the relief in his expression until his gaze settled on the deep purple bruises on her neck.

Before anyone else could react, Tobi had placed her hand on Micah's arm. "Micah, she is already frightened and injured. Please be careful. You are my friend and I don't want you to make a mistake." When he looked down at her, Jax saw the fire in Micah's gaze immediately start to cool. Tobi was definitely going to keep the West brothers on their toes. When she seemed satisfied that Micah had calmed down, she took her small hand from his arm and turned to Gracie. "Sweetheart, you are in wonderful hands. I'm going to step outside so Dr. Brian has room to work. If you need anything please send Micah or Jax to get me." Jax appreciated that Tobi hadn't given Gracie a chance to stop her, she had simply turned and walked from the room.

His first impression of the tiny blonde had been that she was reckless, but now he could see she had just been frightened for her friend. Her loyalty had just gone a long way in earning his respect and he made a note to tell her as much. First he wanted to help the doctor find out as much as he could about her friend's injuries.

KENT SHOOK HIS head as he settled Tobi on his lap. He'd sat on a ridiculously narrow sofa in the hallway outside the club's first aid station. She had squeaked when the plug pushed in deep and he wondered how much longer they should leave it in. Deciding it was the only thing keeping him from upending her and paddling her ass he let his concern about the plug go. "Honest to God, love, I don't know whether to beat your ass or hug you. You took off running from your Masters and called me by my first name inside the club's main room. Then you called me a big lug as you tried to move out of my hold. But the worst of it was putting yourself in danger by stepping in front of a car that was approaching rapidly. Fuck. I don't even want to consider what would have happened if Jax hadn't gotten to you when he did. I swear I'll never tease him about his damned monkey arms again."

Tobi's face flushed bright red and Kent knew she was just now realizing how inappropriate her behavior had been. "Oh my God in heaven. What have I done?" Her green eyes immediately filled with tears and Kent could see the shame in them. When she tried to get off his lap he stilled her. "Please, just let me go. I'm so sorry. I've embarrassed you in front of your friends and club members, and I'm completely humiliated that I was so disrespectful. I was so worried about Gracie that I completely lost focus on everything else." By the time she had finished speaking her tears were streaking down flushed cheeks, but Kent could hear the sincerity in her voice.

"Sit still for a minute and let me get a handle of my frustration before we talk about this. I know that I have to address the behavior, but right now I'm worried about your sweet friend and I am anxious to hear Micah's report before I make any decisions that we both might regret." Being a Dominant was all about what was best for the submissive and in Kent's opinion, and right at this moment, he knew his ability to make a clear decision was being clouded by his anger. A Dom that made emotional rather than rational decisions was dangerous and Kent wasn't going to take any chance of making that mistake.

From the bits and pieces they had gathered about Tobi's childhood, it had been filled with loss and abuse, but they didn't have all the details yet. He and Kyle had talked over the ramifications of that kind of upbringing when they'd been mapping out a strategy to make Tobi their own and they'd agreed that punishments would have to be kept to a minimum until she trusted them enough to feel safe and secure. Her attempt to get off his lap and leave told him that she was already anticipating being rejected, so they were going to have to proceed carefully. On the one hand, she already knew that she'd made a huge mistake and she also knew there would be consequences. But on the other hand, she still didn't understand that punishments wiped the slate clean. They were meant to reinforce lessons not be purely punitive. He knew it would take time for Tobi to understand they not only wanted her, but they liked and respected her as well.

For several seconds Kent just held Tobi on his lap and tried to rein in his anger. By the time Kyle stepped in front of him, he finally felt like he wasn't going to explode. "Kitten, you have gotten yourself in some trouble. We'll deal with that later. Right now what you need to know is that our guys lost the car that was chasing Gracie. It was a black SUV with tinted windows so they didn't get a good look at the driver. And before you ask, there wasn't a license plate on the vehicle either." He had already sent a couple of guys to Gracie's apartment to check out things and pick up a few things for her. They were hoping her apartment key was on the key ring she'd left in her car's ignition so they wouldn't draw attention to the fact she wasn't returning home tonight by speaking with the super. In that neighborhood, that kind of information was probably an open invitation to every two-bit thief for miles.

Watching Tobi sit on Kent's lap, Kyle could feel the tension radiating off her. He knew it wasn't all from her worries about Gracie because she had to know she'd made several big mistakes. He didn't doubt she was worrying about the consequences of her actions as well as how her friend was doing. He ran his fingers through her hair and smiled down at her. "Kitten, we'll deal with it. I'm sure my brother will be lighting up your beautiful ass at some point in the very near future. You already know you've left us no choice but to punish you. And we won't deal with it by walking away, that isn't what we want and it certainly isn't what you need."

Kent was glad to hear Kyle reiterate what he'd already told Tobi because she would need to hear it again and again before she truly believed they weren't going to send her packing at the first sign of trouble. In a lot of ways she reminded him of a fragile bird with a broken wing. Even though he loved her fire and passion, he wanted to help her learn to direct both emotions so they didn't come back and bite her in the ass. When he wrapped his arms tightly around her and hugged her for long seconds Kent felt her relax. It was if she had been waiting for that reassurance and he was grateful he'd been able to give it to her.

Kyle sat beside him and pulled her onto his own lap. "Come here, kitten. I need to feel your heart beating against mine. You scared the shit out of me with that stunt you pulled outside. Don't ever do that again." Kent could hear the emotion in his brother's voice and understood it completely. His own heart had nearly stopped when Tobi had stepped into the car's path. All three men had been trained to assess danger in less than the time it took to blink and they'd all known she'd misjudged the distance and angles. Even now, just thinking about what could have happened made him shudder.

When Micah stepped out of the exam room several minutes later his jaw was set and his eyes flashing fire. He pulled a chair up in front of Kyle and Tobi before leaning forward and clasping his hands together. "Tobi, have you spoken to your brother since the fire at your apartment?"

Kent could see the question surprised Tobi as much as it had both he and Kyle. "No, I haven't. I've been stalling because I just didn't want to answer all of his questions and deal with his condescending comments." Kent watched as realization washed over her expression and it went from confused to disbelief to mortification in just seconds. "Oh my God, please tell me my brother isn't involved in this. He knew Gracie and I were friends, but I can't imagine him hurting her. I know that sounds naïve but it's not what you think. Richard is a pansy-ass. He wouldn't know how to be physically intimidating. He is accustomed to being verbally abusive, that's a given, but I can't see him trying to choke Gracie."

"Is it possible he might be working with Chris Feldman?" Kent felt Tobi's entire body stiffen and her respiration rate was steadily increasing. He was actually concerned she was going to have a panic attack and for several seconds she just seemed to be trying to pull her thoughts together.

"I don't know. I suppose it's possible. They met once that I know of and they seemed to get on all right, but I attributed that to the fact they are both ruthlessly ambitious. I suppose I assumed that meant they understood each other." They all watched as Tobi seemed to center herself again. And this time when she looked up there was a fire in her eyes that hadn't been there before. Jax had stepped into the hall and was leaning against the doorframe listening intently as Tobi continued, "Why are you asking me these questions? And don't even think about lying to me, Micah. I know you are a Dom and we're at the club, but we're friends and I hope we have enough respect for one another that you won't insult my intelligence by trying to deceive me. If my brother or Chris is either one responsible for the harm to Gracie...well, I'm going to need help with a couple of things."

Kyle turned her face to his and asked, "What will you need help with, kitten?"

"I'll need an alibi and help hiding the bodies." Kent saw Kyles's grin a split second before all four of them burst out laughing.

Jax was the first one to regain control and speak, "Damn—I like her. You two ass jacks did good. Sweet cheeks, if you need an accomplice don't you hesitate to call me."

Chapter Seventeen

TOBI FELT A little better after speaking with Gracie and getting her sweet friend settled in the guesthouse that she had been using. Gracie had explained to Jax how she'd been accosted in front of her building as she was returning from work. The man had grabbed her from behind and demanded to know where Tobi was staying and what she'd told the police about the fire. He had mentioned hurting Tobi's sister-in-law, but hadn't mentioned her brother and that had seemed odd to everyone but Tobi.

Tobi had quickly explained that anyone who knew her very well knew she preferred her sister-in-law, Stacey, to her brother, Richard. Tobi also pointed out that if Chris or Richard wanted to threaten her, hurting Gracie or Stacey would be exactly what they would use.

Jax had stayed with Gracie when Kyle and Kent finally pulled Tobi from the small cabin. Gracie had been curled up in the large man's lap sleeping peacefully. As they walked along the lighted path back to the club Tobi started to get nervous, knowing that her day of reckoning was coming quickly. She was torn between wanting to stay quiet in hopes it all blew over and apologizing again. Deciding the ostrich theory had the most merit, Tobi kept still and sent up several prayers to saints she'd never prayed to before. She hoped they might take pity on her since they wouldn't have heard all her lame excuses before.

"Kitten, I can practically hear the wheels in your head spinning. What are you thinking about?" Kyle had stopped at one of the small alcoves in the gardens behind the club and turned to face her.

Oh brother, you are in so deep, Tobi. How could you get yourself in such a batch of pickle fudge anyway? Your mouth, that's how. Hell it's always your mouth. Boy oh boy, you can't lie for shit either and why would you even bother because they both have that damned built in b/s detector. Well frack a feathered flamingo.

As soon as she looked up into their smiling faces she knew she'd been speaking out loud. "Well fuck me. I just never learn." She knew her cursing had probably just thrown gas on the fire but really, she didn't think she could get in much deeper so it didn't seem to matter at this point.

Kyle was shaking his head and chuckling. "Honest to God, I understand our dads' frustration now. You are a handful, kitten. And it's sure easy to see why mom likes you. Christ she's called every day—at least once—to make sure Kent and I aren't screwing this up." Tobi felt her jaw fall open and had to make a conscious effort to close her mouth so she didn't look like a fool.

"Your mom calls and checks on me. Why? I mean...well, she seems like a perfectly nice woman, but we barely know each other. We've only spent a little time together. I can't imagine she could really care about me. Why would she care about me? After all, that doesn't really make any sense does it? If you think—"

"Kitten, stop stalling and answer my question." Kyle's question has suddenly become a demand and he was right, she had been stalling. But it had gotten to be harder to think up things to say than it would be to just blurt out the truth so she was actually kind of relieved.

She took a deep breath and outlined the stone she was standing on with her bare toe before finally looking up. "Well, I was deciding if the ostrich theory or begging for forgiveness was the best plan."

This time Kent chuckled. "Brother, remind me to thank our dads for not strangling our mom." He stepped forward and kissed Tobi on the forehead. "Love, the sooner you figure out that you aren't in charge when it comes to what happens in the club, the easier your life is going to be. Outside of sex, the club, and play, we'll all be equal partners. But we'll pull rank on you every single time you try to top from the bottom, sweetness." Tobi was pretty sure that was an exaggeration, but she was equally convinced now wasn't the time to point it out.

They'd explained topping from the bottom to her earlier in the week and she hadn't really ever figured it would apply to her, but now it was crystal clear that was exactly what she had been trying to do. By attempting to figure out the best way to *control* the situation, she was indeed trying to take charge.

"Kitten, I can tell by the look on your face that you've just had an 'aha' moment." Kyle's voice gave away the fact he wasn't angry with her and she let out the breath she hadn't even realized she was holding. "Now, even though we had something else entirely planned for you in the main room in a few minutes, we now have to address the issue of your misbehavior earlier this evening. Unfortunately you decided to act out in front of several of the club's strictest members and I don't doubt for a minute they are up there waiting to see if we are going to follow through and punish you in a way they will find suitable."

It was dim in the area where they were standing, but Tobi didn't have any trouble interpreting the expression on

Kyle and Kent's' faces. She'd backed them into a corner and they were now stuck in a classic lose-lose situation. Suddenly her trepidation shifted from worry about what they would do to her to feeling horrible for letting them down. "I'm really sorry I've put you in this situation. I didn't think about the consequences for you or myself. I've let you both down and that is the part that bothers me the most. Do whatever you need to do to save face with your members and I'll just accept it with as much grace and dignity as I can." She didn't even realize she'd dropped her gaze to the ground until Kent used his fingers to lift her chin.

He studied her face for several minutes before nodding to his brother. "Let's get this done. I don't like it hanging over any of our heads." When they reached the back door of the club Kent stopped her when she was a step above him and turned her so they were almost eye-to-eye. "Tobi, do you trust us?"

"Yes, Sir. I trust you both." She had tried to sound strong but she knew her words had sounded shaky, but at least they'd been completely sincere.

"That's all we're asking for. Trust us, no matter what you see or hear when we go into the club keep your head down and don't respond to anyone but one of your Masters, clear?" When she nodded, he pulled her forward and kissed her hard. Tobi assumed she'd pushed his control to the very edge and he was setting the tone for what was to come, but the longer he kissed her the more she decided it had been about something else entirely. He was trying to tell her how important she was and he was trying to drive the message in before they stepped through the door and everything changed.

Kyle pulled her close and kissed her with the same fervor, but there was a bit more desperation in his. Her eyes filled with tears and when Kyle felt them against his cheek he pulled back and raised a brow in question. "Kitten?"

"I just want to get this over with because then maybe you can forgive me for messing up so badly or at least I can start trying to regain the ground I've lost with you this evening."

He smiled and kissed her tear-streaked cheeks and then pulled her along behind him, "Come on. The sooner this is over the happier we will all be."

KYLE DIDN'T REMEMBER a time he'd been more reluctant to do something he knew was necessary and right. He and Kent were caught in that proverbial spot between a rock and a hard place. If they didn't punish Tobi for her behavior they'd destroy the trust of every member of their club because the word would spread quickly to every member whether or not they were here tonight. It was also important that Tobi knew their word was golden and something she could always depend on, and they had explained the rules to her a couple of times during the previous week so she knew her actions had consequences. Sighing to himself as they stripped her and bound her to the St. Andrew's cross, Kyle sent up a silent prayer they weren't making a huge mistake.

The small stage had a backdrop that was a series of faceted mirrored tiles and he caught the terrified look in her eyes as she watched the crowd gathering around them. What she didn't know was that most of the people watching were likely more curious because he and Kent never played in this room than they were about seeing her punishment. The fact they had secured her in such a public location was going to attract a lot of attention even if the crowd didn't all know what had happened earlier. Stepping over to the cabinet where supplies were kept, he picked up the black silk scarf and stepped in front of her. "Kitten, I'm going to blindfold you because you are going to get yourself in more trouble by meeting the gazes of those watching. Close your eyes, baby."

After he'd tied the cloth over her eyes he saw her muscles relax fractionally and barely heard her whispered "thank you" before he stepped away. He stepped back and kissed the end of her nose before moving up to the edge of the stage.

"Some of you may have been witness to our sub's misbehavior earlier this evening. My brother and I intend to deal with that misbehavior now. But before we do that, I'd like to remind you that everyone makes mistakes and I want you to know that Tobi's only mistake was caring more about getting to her injured friend than about the consequences she is now facing for her behavior." Several Doms and subs had been listening with almost gleeful expressions and he was pleased to see several of those smiles dim at his explanation.

Kent had stepped in front of Tobi and placed his palm over her cheek. "What is your safe word, Tobi?"

"It's red, Sir."

"And when are you supposed to use it?" Kyle could hear the strain in Kent's voice and knew they had to get this over with quickly for all their sakes.

"If the pain is so unbearable that I can't take it anymore or if I can't take things emotionally any longer, Sir." Kyle heard the catch in her words and knew she was already starting to come apart so he needed to get her mind refocused quickly.

The first swat with the paddle hadn't been hard enough to really be painful, but it certainly would have surprised her and as her yelp confirmed. "Don't tense your muscles or it will just hurt more." Kyle was sure Kent's words were lost on her and she certainly would have felt pain from the second swat. Kyle had chosen a broad paddle to warm her up because it looked wicked but actually spread the impact over the entire surface so the pain was much lower than it looked or sounded like it would be.

He continued swatting her until her ass cheeks were both bright red and hot to the touch. Even though he knew by the shuddering of her shoulders that she was crying, she hadn't made a sound after the first swat. He hated how she was holding the emotion inside, and he was even more worried about *why* she was doing it. Newbie subs often thought they were making their Dom proud if they held everything in when in fact the opposite was actually more accurate. He wanted her to understand that grace and dignity during a punishment are about learning the lesson and accepting the punishment. She didn't have to be silent to learn, hell, she actually hadn't even needed the paddling to learn because she had already known what she'd done wrong. Her guilt wasn't about her actions per se, but rather it stemmed from the fact she wanted to please them and knew she hadn't. It was that desire to please that was at the very heart of submission. They had already witnessed her stoic response to a punishment and Kyle worried that not exploring the reaction was about to come back and bite them in the ass in a very big way.

Kyle wished Tobi had more experience so she'd understand that Doms wanted subs to give them everything and that meant both the good and the bad. Submission is about handing everything that you are over to a person you trust enough to catch you when you fall. In his opinion, a Dom's job is to coach and guide the sub so they can reach a place where they feel secure enough to be themselves. That security is only attainable when the submissive knows clear to their soul there will be someone behind them no matter what. Sure he and Kent knew plenty of Dominants who got off on the power they wielded over their submissive, but that wasn't what it was about for them.

Kent had been standing off to the side warming up his arm and had timed his practice lashes with Kyle's swats so Tobi hadn't been alarmed by the sound of the single-tailed whip cracking. Kyle set the paddle aside and moved over to stand in front of Tobi. He took her tear-stained cheeks in his hands and pushed the blindfold up so he could look into her eyes and more accurately gauge her responses. His body was large enough that he was blocking her view of Kent and the crowd that was now almost ready to cheer at the thought of Tobi being whipped for their viewing pleasure. Kyle was literally almost physically ill at the thought of what they were about to do. He hoped like hell Kent pulled the lashes because he wasn't sure Tobi was ready for that level of pain. When he'd run his fingers through her sex he'd found she wasn't wet at all and that concerned him because it indicated that her body was only processing the sensations as pain and even though it was supposed to be a punishment, he had hoped to give her a release before they finished the scene.

"Kitten, do you want to use your safe word?" Kyle watched as she blinked several times as if she were trying to process his words, but he knew from experience she wasn't anywhere close to subspace. "Tobi? Did you hear the question?"

"Yes, I heard the question, Sir. But, aren't you finished?

Oh God, is there more?" The bleak tone of her voice tore at his heart and he nearly called off the scene at that point. The expression on his face must have alerted Kent there was a problem because he dropped the whip and was at her side in an instant.

Kyle looked at her for long seconds before answering, "No, that wasn't all. You are supposed to get three lashes with the single tail whip but I'm not sure you can take that now."

She started shaking from her core and suddenly her entire body was being racked by nearly silent sobs. He could barely make out the words she was whispering, "No, no, I can't do this again. I don't ever want to do this again. It's just like it always was, a big piece of wood hitting me over and over and over. Please just get it over with now because I won't ever walk in this room again without remembering what has happened here tonight." Tobi's eyes were glazed, her pupils constricted and their movements frantic in a way Kyle had never seen before. He knew her father had used a lot of corporal punishment after her mother had died, but he hadn't known he'd used a wooden paddle. Christ, how irresponsible could they have been? They hadn't even discussed the punishment with her in advance and that might have given them a heads up to the trip wire they'd just stumbled into.

Kyle was quickly unbuckling her and when he looked up at Kent, he simply flashed the sign for "doc" and watched his brother pivot and move quickly off the stage. By the time Kyle had finished unbuckling Tobi, Regi was already at his side holding open one of the club's soft blankets. He nodded his thanks and wrapped it around Tobi just as she collapsed into his arms. Kyle was worried, and starting to become increasingly alarmed because Tobi's eyes were wide open but he knew she wasn't seeing a thing, and her total silence was absolutely haunting. After her initial sobbing and words, it seemed like she had just completely shut down emotionally. He fought back the anger he felt at his own arrogance and he wished like hell he'd listened to his gut feelings earlier and called this whole cluster fuck off.

Chapter Eighteen

Kent sat in the small chair he positioned in the shadows of the master suite's bedroom and just watched Tobi as she slept alone in the enormous bed they'd shared with her so many times over the past week. After they'd rubbed anesthetic cream into her battered behind, he and Kyle settled her in the bed they'd hoped to share with her for the rest of their lives. Right now, he didn't hold out much hope they were going to be granted that opportunity. He and Kyle were both terrified they'd broken something in her during their scene last night and neither of them was convinced they hadn't damaged a part of her soul they would never be able to heal. How had they been so presumptuous? How had they missed all the signs? How had they ignored all their own teaching and failed to ask questions that were critical, particularly when they had already known bits and pieces of her background? How had they managed to put their own reputations as Doms and the owners of the club above the needs of the woman they had both fallen in love with?

He was grateful that both Brian Bennett and Kirk Evans had both still been in the club and had come up to the apartment to evaluate Tobi's condition. She had been virtually catatonic and both physicians had agreed that she'd had some kind of psychotic break and hadn't hesitated to sedate her. Kyle had called Jax to see if Gracie would answer a few questions about Tobi's background, and when he had relayed what had happened all Kyle heard was Jax's cursing before he snapped "on our way" and disconnected the phone. Kent had gone down to meet them and Gracie had practically crawled up his ass during the short ride upstairs in the small elevator. Damn, Jax and Micah were going to have to be careful with that one or she might end up turning the tables on them.

Kyle had been reluctant to leave Tobi's side, but Brian agreed to sit with her while the rest of them talked quietly in the kitchen. Gracie's voice was raspy and strained from her injuries, but she managed to explain the only reason she knew the details of Tobi's childhood was the two of them had shared a couple of bottles of cheap wine one night, and Tobi had finally opened up. Gracie told them Tobi had recounted how her dad had often used her pantyhose to tie her to large nails in the wall and then he would beat her with a wide piece of unfinished wood until he ran out of steam or she passed out. By the time Gracie had finished she'd been crying for her friend and weaving on her feet. Jax had explained how they had given her painkillers earlier as he'd picked her up and cuddled her against his chest before handing her off to Micah.

"Baby, you need to rest." Micah's words were soft and Kent had watched as the two men cared for Gracie and he hoped like hell they learned from the mistakes he and Kyle had made with Tobi. Micah turned to him and said, "We're going to take her back to our cabin so we can make sure she rests. I'm worried about her staying alone after she's taken the pain meds. Obviously they are hitting her pretty hard." Kent and Kyle both thanked Gracie for her help and kissed her on the forehead before bidding their friends good night before returning to Tobi.

Kirk had listened to Gracie's story and he'd encouraged them to remember how strong Tobi must be to have survived so much trauma. "Don't give up on what you want this relationship to be. Tobi is smart and obviously very resilient. Give her time to heal, but don't let her forget how important she is to you both." After they'd gone back in the bedroom to check on her, both Brian and Kirk assured them that she would sleep for several more hours. They promised to return later the next morning with more meds and to check on Tobi after she was awake.

Before the two men left, Brian gripped his arm and spoke quietly, "This doesn't have to break her you know. It may force her to confront some issues from her past that she'd rather leave buried, but she could well end up stronger in the end as a result of this. Don't assume the worst. The best healing balms in the world are compassion and patience." Kent had nodded his understanding and watched as their friends made their way out of the bedroom. Kent really hoped that Regi gave the two doctors a chance because he truly believed they were exactly what their resident tigress needed.

Settling back into his chair, Kent knew that watching Tobi sleep wasn't going to solve the problem of what they should do next, but he couldn't seem to take his eyes off her. He felt his brother stir beside him and noticed that his phone lit up. When he glanced at Kyle's screen he couldn't help but cringe when he saw their mom's name. Kyle cursed softly and quickly made his way out of the room to take the call. Kent had actually considered calling their parents earlier, but the simple truth was he didn't know how on earth he could explain how they'd made such a series of horrible decisions.

Kent knew by the expression on Kyle's face when he

returned to the room the conversation hadn't gone well. Running his hand over his face in frustration, he wondered what their mom was going to do because it was safe to assume she wasn't going to sit back and wait for them to fix things. For some reason she had taken a serious shine to Tobi from the moment they had met. Their mom had dropped by a couple of afternoons during the past week to visit and the two of them had enjoyed tea up on the rooftop patio. Both Kyle and Kent knew their mother had an amazing track record when it came to seeing into the hearts of those around her, and she was determined to have Tobi as a daughter-in-law. That had certainly been his and Kyle's plan as well—until... He wasn't even going to think about that at the moment. Right now he just wanted to watch the sleeping angel in their bed and hope that his own guardian spirit was willing to step in once again and pull his bumbling ass out of the fire.

KYLE WASN'T SURE he'd ever heard his mother as angry as she had just been on the phone. Of all the nonsense he and Kent had gotten themselves into over the years, he had never heard her sound as disappointed in them as she had when he'd finally calmed her down enough to talk with her for a few minutes. And as much as he hated the fact she was mad as a wet hen, it had been his dad Dean's disappointment that had hurt the most. Dad Dell was passionate and full of fire like their mom, so fiery reactions weren't all that uncommon from them. But the family patriarch, Dean West, was the logical, cool head who always prevailed in the midst of any storm. To hear the censure in their dad's voice as he pointed out each and every wrong decision he and Kent had made had cut Kyle to the quick.

Running his hand through his hair, he pulled a chair up alongside Kent and collapsed into it. Never taking his eyes off Tobi, he spoke softly, "Well that was fun. *Christ*. Thanks a lot for all your support by the way. Asshole." Kent chuckled quietly but it sounded empty even to his own ears.

"Tell me." Kent knew they couldn't hope to get off without some kind of intervention on their mom's part. He just hoped it didn't happen too soon, he was beyond exhausted but knew his mind wasn't going to shut down enough to sleep for hours yet.

"She'll be here in a few hours. To say that mom and dad Dell are bouncing off the walls is an understatement. Even dad Dean is pissed as hell." Kyle knew Kent would hear his not so thinly disguised guilt and sadness because it was probably a reflection of his own feelings. "Hearing him tell me how disappointed he is in the both of us was the second lowest moment of my life. I hope like hell that nothing ever makes me feel the gut-wrenching emptiness that I felt when Tobi looked into my eyes and there was nothing there. Seeing her beautiful green eyes vacant felt like someone had gutted me. I could have lived with losing her—maybe. But knowing we'd damaged her fragile soul is destroying me." Kyle felt nothing but desolation as he remembered that moment.

Kyle hadn't taken his eyes off Tobi while he'd been speaking to Kent, and he was surprised to see her hand reach out toward them and open with her palm up. Looking at Kent, he raised his brow in question. They stood and moved to the edge of the bed and sat carefully so they were both angled toward her. When Kyle took her small hand into his own she closed his fingers in her hold and pulled his hand to her chest and sighed. He knew it wasn't a huge gesture, but he hoped like hell it was the sign he'd been praying for. She hadn't opened her eyes but her whispered "please stay" was music to his ears.

He moved so he was laying alongside her on top of the quilt they'd covered her with as Kent moved around the bed and snuggled up against her back so she was spooned in between them. Leaning forward, Kyle pressed his lips against her forehead and held them there for long moments before pulling back. "Always," was all he could manage to speak around the lump that had formed in his throat.

Chapter Nineteen

IT HAD BEEN three days since the disaster in the club's main room and Kent and Kyle were still coddling her as if she was an invalid. They hadn't even let her step foot out of their apartment and Tobi had been perilously close to going stark raving mad. So when Lilly West suggested a shopping trip to Austin, she'd leapt at the chance for some fresh air. Lilly had been the one point of calm in the storm that had surrounded Tobi the past three days. Kent and Kyle had been supportive and attentive in every way. But as Doms their perspective was entirely different.

She and Lilly had spent a lot of time talking about everything that had happened. Lilly had answered every question Tobi had asked her with an openness that surprised and impressed Tobi. She had even answered some questions Tobi had been too embarrassed to ask, Lilly had just laughed when Tobi had blushed at the detailed information. Lilly had been understanding about Tobi's fears of any impact play involving wood assured her there were still many options for BDSM play.

"Did you have anything special in mind to buy today, Tobi?" Lilly's question brought Tobi's attention back to the fact they were just minutes from the first exits that would lead into Austin's various shopping areas.

"No, not really. I don't actually have any money to spend, well not much anyway. I have only gotten paid once so far and I put most of that toward catching up my student loans. I fell pretty far behind while I was only working part-time." Tobi had fallen so far behind she hadn't thought she could ever catch up. And sure, she hated the effect it was going to have on her credit rating, but mostly she just hated not meeting her obligations. She mentally winced when she thought about what Richard was going to say when he got wind of it.

When Kyle and Kent first presented her with their salary offer she had been completely stunned. It hadn't taken her long to mentally calculate how quickly she could wipe out the entire debt. It had been even sweeter when she considered she had minimal living expenses since she was living in the smallest of their guesthouses. She had barely resisted her urge to dance around their office naked she'd been so overjoyed with their offer. Laughing to herself at the realization how they would have loved that, she remembered hearing her mama use that expression when she'd been just a little girl. She hadn't thought about that saying in a long time and wondered if her mom hadn't just touched her soul for that particular memory to pop up.

"Well the boys sent a rather nice wad of cash with me with very specific instructions that we are to spend it all on you today. So, you need to think about where you'd like to go or I'm going to decide." The wicked grin Lilly gave her made Tobi laugh out loud.

"Oh Lord, I can only imagine what you might think up. I guess we could hit Walmart, I could use some shampoo and my jeans are pretty ratty."

Lilly looked at her and frowned. "If we take this much cash into Walmart we'll have to rent a truck to get all the stuff home. Nope, this kind of shopping calls for boutiques, Tobi. I think I know just the place to start." Tobi watched as Lilly wove in and out of traffic like a Formula 500 driver and almost as fast. *Cripes, the woman drives like a demon. Wonder if her husbands ever let her drive.* "You know, you'll get a cramp in your hand if you don't lighten up on that door handle. And don't worry, you'll get used to my driving soon enough." Personally, Tobi wasn't convinced, but she didn't want to distract Lilly from avoiding cars, pedestrians, and bicyclists as they raced down the street.

The two of them spent the next several hours spending obscene amounts of money on a variety of clothing Tobi was convinced she didn't need. Even though she'd agreed to continue working at Prairie Winds and that was going to mean she had to at least walk through the club's main room, she still wasn't planning to play there ever again so club wear seemed a huge waste of money to her.

While they were enjoying a late lunch Tobi's phone rang. Digging it out of her bag, she glanced at the screen and groaned when she saw her brother's name. "Hi Richard, what's up?" Lilly could obviously hear her brother's ranting and raving because her expression had quickly changed from relaxed interest to incredibly annoyed in less than thirty seconds. Tobi tried to calm her brother down but wasn't having much luck when he suddenly hung up. Looking at the phone and shrugging her shoulders, she dropped it back in her purse. "Well, that was odd. He usually just sends me nasti-grams or demands that I meet him at his place so he can rage at me in person when he doesn't think I'm living up to his public image."

Lilly leaned forward and took Tobi's hand in hers, "Do you think we should head back? Could he be a problem?"

The truth was, Tobi didn't really know because Richard had been shouting about it being all her fault that Stacey was involved, and that hadn't made any sense to her at all. But the hair on the back of Tobi's neck was sticking up and even though she wasn't sure exactly why, she wasn't willing to ignore the feeling either. It would be one thing to face her brother alone, but she sure didn't want Lilly West exposed to his rude behavior. "I don't know, but I'm ready to head back if you are. I'd like to use the restroom before we go though...you know, so your driving doesn't scare me too badly. It would be embarrassing to go back with wet drawers." She loved the fact that Lilly could give as good as she got with teasing and the look of mock indignation on her face sent Tobi into a fit of giggles.

LILLY WATCHED TOBI walk down the hall to the ladies lounge and then quickly pulled out her own phone and dialed the number that would send the call to both of her husbands' phones. That little techno-feature had been one of their gifts to her last Christmas and she loved it because it had always seemed that regardless which of her men she dialed first she ended up needing to call the other in order to get an answer. She quickly explained the situation to Dell and asked him to let their sons know that they might be coming in "hot and fast."

Dell had laughed, "No more spy thriller movies for you for a while, darlin'. And just so you know, my love, you *always* come hot and fast." He'd hung up and she smiled at her phone before putting it away and hoped she wasn't blushing at his blatantly sexual teasing. Who knew that the three of them would still be enjoying such an active sex life after all these years? Lilly was sure that it was largely due to their BDSM lifestyle and she was sure her sons would find the same with Tobi as soon as they got past this bump in the road.

Tobi had certainly come a long way in the past couple of days. Lilly had spent a lot of time explaining various aspects of their lifestyle. She hadn't held back her frustration with the mistakes her sons had made with Tobi, but she had also assured the younger woman that Doms are just like everyone else in that they make mistakes. Lilly knew Tobi wasn't holding the incident against Kent or Kyle, but she also worried that Tobi wouldn't be able to get past her fear so she could reengage in the lifestyle that would fulfill her.

As she drove the two of them back to Prairie Winds, Lilly noticed a dark colored SUV with tinted windows that appeared to be following them. She deliberately took an exit that wasn't on their route just to test her theory and when it followed, she knew they needed to call for help. Both of her husbands had insisted she take an evasive driving course a few years ago designed to teach people how to avoid being a target and she was suddenly very thankful for their foresight.

"Tobi, grab my phone. Press and hold down the number one key, when it starts to ring let me know." Tobi did exactly as she was told and Lilly pressed the button on her steering wheel that connected the car's audio system to her phone.

Dean answered and she was grateful he had picked up so quickly, "Hi gorgeous, how's your shopping trip going? Buy anything for me to tear off of you?" She couldn't help but smile at his flirting and Tobi's instant blush.

"I did indeed, Master. But right now we have a problem. We're being followed. Black SUV with tinted windows. Could you please call the boys and Micah? We're just pulling back on the highway and we'll be heading west again in a minute. Micah can track my car." She could hear him speaking with Dell and was glad they were together.

"We're on it, love. Stay on the phone with me while Dell calls Micah. Is Tobi okay?" Dean's voice was full of concern and Lilly knew the eldest of her husbands already had a soft spot in his heart for Tobi.

"She's fine, although she seems a bit uncomfortable with my driving for some reason." Lilly laughed at Tobi's blush and Dean's snort on the other end of the connection.

"Well, that is baffling isn't it, sweetheart?" Lilly could hear the affection in Dean's voice and glancing at Tobi she was happy to see her attempt to lighten the mood a bit seemed to have been successful.

KYLE HAD BEEN almost frantic when his dad had called to say they were tracking his mom and Tobi because they were being followed. The description of the vehicle matched the one that had followed Gracie to Prairie Winds, so there wasn't much doubt that whoever was tailing them knew where the women were headed. Jax had made sure Gracie was in the main building under Tank's care and then had taken off with Kent, while Micah and Kyle manned the phones and monitored the situation using various surveillance methods, many of which Kyle guessed were probably not entirely legal.

Micah had already alerted Parker Andrews but since the women were already out of the city limits, Parker had been forced to relay the information to law enforcement with county jurisdiction. He had assured Kyle he was leaving his office anyway and heading that direction so he could help in any way he could, and Kyle certainly appreciated his effort. There were several roadside traffic cams along the women's route and Micah had made short work of tapping into that system. They had tried to get a close-up on the driver of the SUV but so far they hadn't had any luck. "My concern is that whoever is driving is going to start feeling desperate and get more aggressive, which will make them careless. Careless people make mistakes, but they also hurt people and there is usually collateral damage." Micah's words echoed Kyle's own thoughts. He had no sooner spoken than the vehicle slammed into the back of his mom's car sending it fishtailing down the highway.

"*Fuck!*" Kyle was on the phone immediately to Jax and Kent to find out their location and give them an update. Just as Kent answered, a large hole appeared in the passenger door of the black SUV and the front tire exploded. The vehicle immediately slid into the ditch, resting nose down with steam coming from under the hood. "Shit, did you see that? Where are they?"

"Not sure, but they have to have been close to your parents' new place because that was the last of the traffic cams. My guess is those holes in the SUV are not a coincidence." Micah was already laughing and Kyle agreed that it looked like his dads had decided a bit of Texas intervention was in order. As the driver's door on the SUV opened the area was inundated with law enforcement vehicles. Kyle watched a slender figure emerge before being pinned to the ground by the officers that had surrounded the vehicle. He was glad to see the driver had been apprehended—but the sight of his mother's car sliding into view did not make him happy at all.

Tobi couldn't believe it when Lilly turned around and headed back toward the car that had just rear-ended them. The call with Dean had gone silent for a couple of seconds and Tobi had wondered if they'd been disconnected. Instead, Dell had come back on and told them the car following them had crashed. Tobi still worried that Lilly was putting herself in danger because some fruitcake didn't like her. "Are you sure we should be here?" Tobi asked as Lilly slid to a stop.

"I want to see who hit us. It's probably the same person who hurt your friend and now tried to get to us. That just plain pisses me off and I want to find out firsthand who is responsible." Tobi found herself scrambling to catch up with the Lilly who was much taller and seemed to have the power walk down to a fine science. "You know if we go straight back to Prairie Winds we'll never find out anything. I swear I love my husbands and sons more than life itself, but sometimes their view of me as defenseless is a very real pain in my ass."

Tobi snorted a laugh because the language was such a contrast to the controlled "lady" that she'd gotten to know the past few days. "Well, I hope you aren't getting me in trouble with Kyle and—" she didn't get to finish her sentence because she was grabbed from behind around the waist and lifted off the ground.

"Kent? Is that what you were asking, sweetness? Oh, you hang around with my mama and I promise you she is going to get you into trouble regularly, my love. But it's part of her charm and we love her despite the fact she doesn't have a lick of sense when it comes to her vulnerability sometimes." She turned her head, met his smiling eyes, and relaxed into his hold when she realized he wasn't angry with her.

Jax had wrapped his hand around Lilly's upper arm to stop her or Tobi figured the other woman would have stomped right in among the officers who appeared to be hauling the driver and another person back up the ditch's steep slope. As they walked toward her, Tobi could easily identify Chris by his well-rounded shape and arrogant walk. But it was the slender driver whose wisps of blonde hair seemed to be escaping around the ball cap she was wearing that took her breath away.

"Stacey?" Tobi asked as the group started to walk past them. "Why? Why would you do this?" She was so stunned she could barely speak and she hoped the anger quickly replaced the feeling of utter betrayal she was feeling because anything would be better than the hole that had blossomed in her heart. Stacey had always been her defender, she had always calmed Richard's frustration, and her sister-in-law had appeared to genuinely like her even when she'd gently tried to prod Tobi into dressing better and finding a more prestigious job. Suddenly it all became crystal clear, it had all just been an act. A very sophisticated manipulation that Tobi hadn't understood because she hadn't been raised in a social class that valued appearance over substance. All the years of insecurity and self-doubt came crashing over her in waves of destruction that rivaled the most devastating hurricanes.

Stacey looked down her nose at Tobi and rolled her eyes. "Richard has so much potential, but you were always an anchor he couldn't let go of. We tried to help you, but you were content to be the trashy sister who would always be mentioned in any story that was done on him once he entered politics. Then you took up with two men...*TWO* men who own a sex club for God sakes. How is your brother supposed to gather the kind of support and donations he needs to make for a successful run for state office with you as baggage?"

The officer who had his arm clamped firmly around Stacey's upper arm gave Tobi a sympathetic smile and pushed her sister-in-law toward the waiting patrol car. Tobi didn't speak. She was too stunned to even move. Everything she had believed about her brother's wife had just been shattered and the pieces turned to dust that drifted away on the southern breeze. The feeling of emptiness that assailed her almost caused her knees to buckle. The years of feeling as if you were never going to be good enough came back in a rush as all the progress she'd made crumbled around her. Tobi didn't doubt for a minute that her brother would back his wife to the end, so she knew she had just lost the last of her family. Feelings of loneliness pressed in on her until she felt one tear slide down her cheek.

Tobi had felt strong arms surround her from behind and she leaned back against Kent and tried to absorb some of his strength. Even though she was surrounded by people who were moving and talking, Tobi wasn't thinking about anything except letting Kent fill a small part of the vast chasm that had formed where her soul had once resided. The image of a bb bouncing around inside a boxcar flashed through her mind. It had always been how her father had criticized her intelligence, telling her that was how tiny her brain was inside her head. She knew the comparison was absurd, but hearing the same litany for years on end, had still caused very real damage.

She didn't know how long she'd stood there lost in

thought but she vaguely remembered Chris Feldman being marched by her and snarling that if she had just listened to him none of this would have happened, before he was shoved on. Blinking to bring everything back into focus, Tobi realized Lilly West was standing in front of her, hands on her slender hips while she tapped the toe of her leather boots against the blacktop.

"Well, it's about time you brought that brilliant mind of yours back online, young lady. I've been talking to you and you looked like you were looking right through me. That just isn't going to do, Tobi. Mothers don't like to be ignored you know." Tobi couldn't help but return Lilly's smile. Tobi knew Lilly had a heart of pure gold and she appreciated her effort, but the pain was still raw and Tobi just wanted to retreat into herself and sleep away the pain. "Oh no you don't. I know that vacant look. You just bring your happy self right back here, Tobi. Pay very close attention to what I'm telling you because I get cranky when I have to tell people the same thing over and over." Tobi felt Kent's chuckle against her back and watched as Dean and Dell West stood to the side nodding their heads, knowing smiles on their faces. "You don't base your self-image on what some spoiled brat with an oversized sense of entitlement says. That isn't where your self-worth is rooted. And that foolishness about family being people who share blood ties is bullsh….um, shampoo as well. Family is all about the people you surround yourself with, people that love you through thick and thin. The folks who aren't afraid to tell you to yank your head out of your ass…ets when you need to hear it."

Tobi felt her cheeks flush at Lilly's matter of fact statements and she was proud of herself for holding back her giggle as Dean and Dell shook their heads at their wife's attempts to cover up her cursing. Lilly hadn't coddled or offered a shoulder to cry on. She'd basically told Tobi to suck it up and move on and it was exactly the type of kick in the pants her own mother would have given her. Tobi stepped out of Kent's embrace and into Lilly's outstretched arms. "Thank you" was all she managed to say because she was suddenly fighting back tears of joy and the light feeling that filled her heart. The joy that filled her was a contradiction considering what she'd just learned, but knowing that she could choose her family was far more important than any of the bile Stacey had just spewed at her.

Lilly hugged her for several long seconds and Tobi couldn't believe the comfort she found in the embrace. She'd been so young when her own mother had died that she had forgotten the safety and sense of security that could be found in a hug. Kent finally pulled her back and picked her up. "Come on, love, time to go home." *Home.* She hadn't really had a home in so long she wasn't sure she fully understood the concept anymore, but suddenly she was very anxious to try.

Chapter Twenty

STANDING IN THE bedroom Tobi shared with Kyle and Kent West, she looked at her reflection in the mirror that Clint and Kimberly Bollinger had given them as an engagement gift. A few days after the incident on the highway with Stacey and Chris, Tobi had traveled to Sealy with Kent and Kyle to meet with Clint and his staff. They'd worked out all the details for the elaborate display racks and shelving she'd envisioned for the forum shops.

Thinking back on the day her sister-in-law and former co-worker had tried to run her and Lilly West off the road, Tobi had to suppress the chill that raced up her spine. She still wondered how those two had managed to team up, but it was unlikely she'd ever know the truth. Her brother had quickly managed to shift all the blame to Chris, and Tobi had to give him credit, he had played the media masterfully. In the end, Richard had made both his wife and sister appear as if they'd been victims of Feldman's insane obsession with Tobi. She hadn't actually spoken to her brother since the shit had hit the fan with his wife, and oddly enough, she just couldn't find it in her heart to care.

When she, Kent, and Kyle had travelled to Sealy, they had spent the better part of an entire day reviewing the designs for all the things E.G.A. Fabrication was going to create for them. She had even gotten to spend some time in their shop. Getting her hands on a plasma cutter and welder for the first time in years had left Tobi almost giddy. When she'd flipped up the helmet Clint had lent her, she knew she was grinning like a kid with a new toy. When she'd looked up at Kent and Kyle they'd been chuckling and shaking their heads indulgently at her. "Guess we know what she wants for Christmas." Kyle's words had been filled with affection and she'd nodded eagerly.

"Most women want kitchen gadgets and jewelry, but not ours. Hell no, she wants boy toys." Kent had winked at her and she'd happily given him a thumbs up before disappearing back behind the helmet. Her skills had been pretty rusty, but the E.G.A. staff had been kind with their observations and guidance. The three of them had joined Clint and Kimberly for dinner and it had been Kimberly who had reminded her that karma was a universal force and that even though it might appear as though her sister-in-law was going to get off scot-free, that wouldn't be the case long term.

Kimberly had leaned over to clasp her hand over Tobi's forearm before assuring her, "Karma never forgets and its timing is always perfect...just watch and see." Tobi had felt a large chunk of her anger break away and she had nodded her understanding. From that moment on, she and Kimberly had become fast friends. Tobi was thrilled the couple would be among the family and friends gathering downstairs for the bonding ceremony, binding her to Kent and Kyle in a way that marriage never could. Oh, she had married Kyle early that morning in a small civil ceremony, but tonight was the meaningful merging of them as a true ménage partnership.

Glancing out the bedroom window, Tobi smiled at the building's large addition. The construction crews had worked almost round the clock so the façade facing the backyard would be finished and provide a beautiful backdrop to their sunset ceremony. They'd broken ground on The Forum several weeks ago and Tobi was continually amazed at the rapid pace the construction had taken. Several of the small shops were nearing completion and on one of his first trips to Prairie Winds, Clint had delivered the mirror she'd been enjoying. Its hidden hinges and wheels made it perfect for bedroom play because it could be positioned anywhere in the room and the five panels could be angled to reflect an infinite number of erotic scenes. The scrollwork along the outside edge was so fine it was hard to believe it had been cut rather than molded. There were cleverly concealed images in the design and the broad base had drawers Kimberly had filled with an assortment of toys and various bottles of lube.

Tobi smoothed her hands over the strapless gown she'd chosen to wear this evening and sighed. The fabric flowed and swirled reminding Tobi of the gowns Disney Princesses wore in all of her favorite children's movies. The color matched her green eyes perfectly and the small crystals sewn in intricate patterns would pick up the light from the zillion or so fairy lights Lilly had strung through the backyard. When they had tested the lighting last night, Toby had been mesmerized and Lilly had been jumping up and down clapping her hands with childlike excitement. And even though Dean and Dell had teased their wife unmercifully about becoming the Clark Griswold of Austin, they'd also been the first to point out an area that they considered "under-emphasized," which Tobi had quickly learned meant they would be adding another thousand lights to that small area of the yard.

Lilly had taken Tobi shopping for dresses to wear to both the civil ceremony and tonight's much more formal event. When Tobi had stepped out of the dressing room in the dress she was now wearing, her future mother-in-law had gasped and immediately started nodding. Lilly's eyes had filled with tears as she watched Tobi swirl around in front of the mirrors. "Oh Tobi, it is absolutely perfect for you. I can't imagine you wearing another dress...not after seeing you in this. And my sons are going to be awfully glad I made them learn ballroom dancing."

She could laugh about it now, but at that moment Tobi had suddenly been completely overcome with terror. *Dancing? Ballroom dancing? Oh shit!* She knew her expression had given her away when Lilly burst out laughing. "Oh Lord, sweetheart, I hope you don't play poker with my husbands or sons, because your face is among the most expressive I've ever seen. So, I'm guessing my mention of formal dance is what has put that look on your face, is that right?"

Tobi nodded frantically before finally finding her voice. "Yes. Oh my, I can two-step...mostly. But I can't do anything else and I don't have enough time to learn because it took me forever to get my two left feet to learn the two-step. I'm not kidding, if there had been a remedial dancing class, I'd have been a shoe in. Damn and double damn, my Texas citizenship was already nearly revoked because it took me so long to learn to two-step. I swear there are Dance Police in Austin and they prowl the clubs and if you can't two-step you are escorted to the borders and promptly shoved out of the Lone Star State. How am I going to do this? And I'll bet I have to wear nice shoes with this dress too, right? Oh Lord, if I wear boots Kent will blow a gasket and I'll get a...well, never mind about that." It had suddenly occurred to her that she was babbling and had nearly talked about her fiancé paddling her ass to his mother. *Damn Tobi, talk about having a run-away mouth. Best be learning to edit before Lilly figures out what a total screw-up you are and warns off her sons.*

When Lilly leaned her head back and roared in laughter, Tobi had just blinked at her in surprise. Tobi looked on as Lilly spent the next several minutes trying to regain her composure. Tobi finally led the cackling woman around the wingback chair she'd been leaning against while she'd been gasping for breath. "Oh Tobi, I can't tell you how much joy you bring into my life. Hearing you chatter away as your mind is spinning out of control reminds me so much of myself at your age. I can see now why Dell and Dean loved listening to me. Hell, I can see how I handed them every bit of inside information they ever needed…and here I thought they were just really insightful."

Lilly's last comment caused Tobi to start giggling and it hadn't taken long before their contagious laughter had spread throughout the entire small bridal shop. After they had returned to Prairie Winds, Dean and Dell West had both helped Tobi polish her dancing skills. When they had pointed out that since she already knew how to two-step, it was an easy transition to most of the other dances she needed to know. Their patience had paid off and by the end of the evening, she was confident she knew the steps and she had even mastered the high heels she planned to wear.

Moving back in front of the mirror, Tobi lifted the hem of her dress and looked at the strappy sandals she was wearing. She had nearly swooned when she'd tried them on, but when she'd looked at the price tag she had promptly set them back on the shelf. Lilly had huffed out a barely edited curse before handing them to the salesman and turned to Tobi with her hands on the hips in a "I'm not taking any guff from you" stance that had silenced Tobi's protests before she'd even had a chance to speak them aloud.

Looking up into the mirror Tobi saw Kent and Kyle both standing behind her. The sight of them in their tuxes had stolen her breath and when she spun around to face them all she could do was gape at them. "Well, brother, I can't remember ever seeing our wife speechless before. Of course she'd only been our wife for a few hours so I guess we aren't slacking too much."

Kent's brilliant smile and sweet words warmed her heart. "You both look...well, you are simply...dashing, yes that's the word. You simply take my breath away. And no matter what ever happens...I want you to know how very much I love you both." Tobi was determined she wasn't going to cry because Gracie had worked too hard making sure her makeup was flawless.

Kyle stepped forward and took her hands in his. His gaze was so focused she was sure he was reading every hope and dream her heart had ever known. When he finally spoke, Tobi could hear the emotion in his voice. "Kitten, we had wondered for so long when we would find you. And truthfully there were a lot of lonely nights when I was worried we wouldn't. Then, remarkably, there you were. Standing in the middle of the highway during a fearsome storm surrounded by lightning strikes and soaking wet...and heart-stoppingly beautiful. Kent and I have made some mistakes with you along the way and I don't doubt that we'll make more. But I want you to know the one thing you can always count on is the fact our love for you is unshakable. We'll support you and protect you, even when you don't really want us to."

"What my brother is dancing around is we'll always have your back, love. Your happiness comes second only to your safety. Now, we have a gift for you before we go downstairs for the ceremony." The sparkle in Kent's eyes told her he was very proud of whatever it was they'd picked out for her, though she couldn't imagine what it could be because they'd showered her with gifts for weeks.

When they each stepped aside Tobi found herself facing a four foot tall framed photo of herself as a young child sitting on her mother's lap. Tobi felt as if all the oxygen had been stripped from her lungs. She remembered seeing the photograph once years ago, but she'd never had a copy even though she had always wished for one. The picture had been taken before he mother's diagnosis and her carefree spirit was easy to see reflected in her bright smile. Her hair was long and only slightly darker in color than Tobi's, but the waves and curls were the same.

Tobi stood in front of the picture for so long that she noticed Kyle and Kent were starting to become restless. When she looked up, glancing between them, she could see the uncertainty in their eyes. "Kitten?" Knowing she'd given them the impression she wasn't thrilled with the gift made her feel like an ungrateful wench. Kent stepped forward and pulled a soft handkerchief from the inside pocket of his jacket and dabbed the tears she hadn't even realized were running down her cheeks.

She leaned forward and kissed him sweetly, pressing her lips against his before repeating the gesture with Kyle. "It's perfect. No one has ever given me a gift that I have loved more or captured my heart more than this one. I really just don't have the words to tell you how much it means to me...and not just that you've obviously restored and enlarged it, and had it beautifully framed. But that you would take the time to seek out a picture from the time in my childhood when everything was right in my world.

That is the true spirit and value of this gift." Tobi could see them both let out sighs of relief and she had to smile to herself, because she would have never guessed they'd be so apprehensive and unsure about pleasing her.

"Well, my love, we wanted to give you something today that would remind you that you can choose the memories you want to hold dear. It seemed an important message as we begin our lives together. You might also want to thank Micah for finding your mom's best friend. Eliza Jessop was thrilled to help us with this and she can't wait to meet you. She and her daughter, Betsy, are downstairs with the rest of our family and friends." Kent's smile lit up his entire face and in an instant Tobi saw a flash of a little boy with that exact same smile and the glimpse of the future stole her breath.

Chapter Twenty-One

Kent knew watching Tobi weave her way through the family and friends as she made her way to where he and Kyle waited was a moment he would never forget. They had intentionally made sure the makeshift aisle wasn't a straight line. It was representative of the fact that no one's life is a straight path to a goal, rather it's an intricate series of stepping-stones through both the good and bad. Kent's poetic notions had often elicited snorts and eye rolling from his brother, but this time Kyle had been fully on board with his observations and plan.

Tobi had been amazingly easy to work with during all the planning of this celebration, telling them time and again she would be thrilled with anything they or their parents planned. The only time she'd demanded a change was during the civil wedding ceremony earlier that morning. Even though she was "technically" marrying Kyle, she had insisted Kent stand by his brother's side and answer all the same questions and repeat the same vows. She had also repeated hers to each of them. She had been determined that he not be left out. He hadn't thought his love for her could grow any deeper until that moment, and he'd suddenly realized there would never be a "bottom or limit" to the amount of love he felt for her.

She wasn't rushing down the aisle and Kent couldn't help the grin he knew was spreading over his face. Tobi was making eye contact and smiling with each person along her path, and she even stopped to hug several. When she finally stepped up on the small stage and turned to face them, Kent could see her eyes were glistening with unshed tears of joy. The ceremony itself had been brief, but the words spoken had sealed their bond in a way marriage vows never could.

The collar Kent had designed was a delicate chain made from fine links of platinum, titanium, and gold. The platinum and titanium represented the strength he and Kyle would bring to their union and the gold was for the beauty and value Tobi contributed. The lock was built into the design and there were diamonds among the links so it sparkled as it reflected the twinkling lights that surrounded them. Sliding the small lock into place as Tobi knelt at their feet had been one of the happiest moments of Kent's life.

Kent's first dance with Tobi was to "Amazed" by Lone Star. He'd chosen that song because he was truly amazed at how quickly everything had changed for him once Tobi entered his life. Pressing her against him made his cock even harder than it had been since they'd walked into the master suite and seen her reflected so beautifully in the black framed mirror. He leaned down and kissed the shell of her ear, "Love, I'll never forget how beautiful you look tonight. You are perfection and knowing that you belong to my brother and me lights a fire in my soul. Tonight you are going to find out exactly what it means to belong to both of us."

They had been waiting to take her together until the time was right. They'd been preparing her for weeks, but tonight they'd show her the joy of a true ménage. He'd felt a shudder move through her at his words, but he knew it was anticipation rather than fear. She'd tried to tempt them several times, including a sexy striptease last night that had earned her an erotic spanking she was probably still feeling today. He had to stifle a laugh as he remembered the surprised look on her face when they'd turned the tables on her after last night's walk through of all today's plans. He hoped she never stopped pushing them because he loved the fact she found such pleasure in pushing the limits as much as they liked reining her in.

As the first strands of "You Had Me at Hello" by Kenny Chesney began, Kent whirled Tobi into Kyle's waiting arms. "Kitten, this song is perfect for us. Even though you didn't technically say hello to me, you had me from the moment I saw you."

Tobi chuckled, "I really should apologize for my behavior that day at some point. But to be honest, it is awfully hard to regret something that brought me to you and Kent. I love your mother for a lot of things, but that was the first." Kyle looked in her eyes and knew he'd never tire of seeing the light that shone in them.

There was something deep in Tobi's heart that was so pure there were times when Kyle felt like he could feel it reaching out to touch his own. Her love was slowly setting his own battered soul back on the right track. Years of military service, much of it in the Special Forces had left their mark on him and even though Kent had been more resilient, he hadn't escaped entirely unscathed either.

Moving around the dance floor with Tobi was almost magical. Their dads had tipped them off that Tobi had been worried about dancing to anything other than two-step music, so he and Kent had been careful when choosing the songs for their first dances. Since all eyes would be on her for these first dances they had wanted to make sure she was comfortable. There would be plenty of time for pushing her into "uncharted territory" later. And it seemed like a good time to remind her of that fact.

"Kitten, did my brother mention we have big plans for you later?" When he heard her sharp intake of breath, he smiled to himself. "Did he describe to you how we will make you come at least twice just to make sure your body is ready? Then, we're going to make sweet love to your body at the same time. One of us will slide into your delectable ass and light up nerve endings you haven't even imagined are there. And then, the other will push into your perfect pussy and you will feel the exquisite fullness that can only come from true ménage loving, kitten. We'll love you forever, never forget that. But tonight is going to be about learning what it means to belong to two Masters." He leaned down and lightly bit that soft spot where her slender neck joined her shoulder before licking the faint imprint his teeth had left. "*Mine*. Mine to love. Mine to protect. Mine to fuck." He smiled to himself when he felt her entire body shudder in response.

The rest of the evening passed in a blur of congratulations and backslapping, but Kyle couldn't take his eyes off his new wife. His gaze seemed to track her and seek her out even when he was speaking with friends and family. He and Kent had watched as she charmed every person she met. The only time she'd let her tears fall had been during her conversation with her mother's best friend and then when Don and Patty had given her their gift. Don had lovingly refinished her cedar chest and Patty had cleaned all the items inside. Watching her appreciation of their gift had left everyone watching in awe. Leaning against the stone wall along the edge of the yard, Kyle heard Kent's soft sigh.

"She's everything we dreamed about—and more. There aren't enough flowers in the world to thank mom for this gift."

"And I'm sure she is going to remind us regularly that she is the reason we found Tobi." Just as Kyle spoke the words he heard dual snorts of laughter from his other side. Turning he saw both his dads leaning against the wall in positions that mirrored his and Kent's.

Dad Dean flashed him a smile that let him know he agreed. "Your mama loves that girl as if she'd given birth to her. You two better watch your p's and q's you know."

"Yep. There are some things that even Dean and I won't be able to save you from and a pissed off mama bear will be one of them. Hell, we won't even try." Dell's laugh did little to hide just how true the words were that he'd just spoken.

Kyle smiled as he glanced between his fathers. He loved them equally, and he nor Kent had ever made any attempt to find out which one of the West brothers had actually fathered them because it just simply did not matter. "Mom has already made that very clear to both of us—more than once. We'll never be able to thank her enough for recognizing how perfect Tobi would be for us."

"And for seeing to it that we had a chance to find it out. Hell, Austin Gardens and Homes never did get their damned interview," Kent laughed.

"They won't now either, not after the way they treated Tobi. Your mama has been spreading the word through her friends. Until they fire Feldman, they won't be getting into any of those folks' homes either." Dean stood and looked carefully at both of his sons. "We've agreed to lease the building at the front of our place to Jax and Micah. Seems they'd like a place closer to Prairie Winds for their business and I think they plan to do some remodeling and make a home there as well."

Kyle and Kent both nodded, Micah had already mentioned their plans to the West brothers. "It seems as if a certain Latin spit-fire has captured their interests." They all laughed because Gracie Santos had been a handful for their two friends from the start. Kyle knew she was sorely testing the patience of both Doms. Gracie had recently agreed to stay in the guest cabin but had still been commuting to the city to work until the small shop where she worked closed its doors. Kyle knew Tobi wanted to hire her to get the forum shops opened, but he didn't know whether or not Gracie had agreed to take the job.

Looking out over the dance floor, Kyle smiled as he watched Jax and Micah handing Gracie off between them. They hadn't let her out of their sight the entire evening. Hell, they'd been reluctant to let her dance with him. Shaking his head, he met Tobi's gaze and when she smiled at him, he felt his heart swell. He and Kent pushed away from the wall at the same instant as if they'd rehearsed the move. "Time to rescue our wife. She looks tired and I do believe she is due some pampering."

Both of their dads laughed out loud before dad Dell smirked at them, "That was just plain lame, son."

"Lord, you'd have thought they'd have learned something about making better excuses after all the years they listened to us make them when we wanted to spend alone time with their mama." Kyle and Kent walked away, leaving their dads laughing behind them. Kyle was sure the two were getting ornerier as they got older and wondered what they'd be like when they finally managed to retire. *Lord help us.*

Chapter Twenty-Two

Tobi stood in the master suite's enormous bathroom and stared at herself in the mirror. The nightgown she was wearing had been a shower gift from Gracie who had promised it would be perfect for her grand entrance into the bedroom on her wedding night. Tobi agreed the pale shade of periwinkle was beautiful and the sparkling slender straps that held the nearly translucent garment up were a lovely distraction, but she was fairly sure they weren't going to be enough to keep her new husbands from shredding it the minute she walked in the room. The very first rule they'd given her when she agreed to move in was that she was never to wear anything in their bed. *But I wanted to look special tonight. I wanted to be able to pretend I'm a beautiful gift that they get to unwrap.* Letting out a soft sigh, Tobi turned toward the door and saw both objects of her affection leaning against the doorframe in identical mirrored poses.

Their features were softened with affection and the light of love shone in their matching dark brown eyes. Tobi loved the way their eyes darkened when they were aroused and the fact they were nearly black now told her how much they appreciated Gracie's gift. She couldn't believe she felt the warmth of a blush spreading up her chest and neck, and in seconds her entire face felt so hot she was sure she was probably practically glowing.

"Kitten, you are most definitely a gift. And we are very much looking forward to unwrapping you." Kyle's voice had already deepened and Tobi loved the fact his words sounded a bit strained.

"Love, Gracie told us that she'd given you something special to wear. We just wanted to make sure you knew it was alright to wear it when you came to us." Tobi let out a breath she hadn't realized she was holding as she moved to clasp their out-stretched hands.

Stepping into the bedroom was like entering a fairy wonderland. There were bouquets of fresh flowers on every available surface and tiny candles were flickering all around. The soft glow of the candles painted the room with an ambiance that made her feel as if she had stepped right into one of her romance novels. The entire room had been transformed in the few minutes she'd been in the bathroom and the fact they'd done it for her simply took her breath away. "Oh my God...it's...well, it's absolutely enchanting. How did you do it so quickly? It's just remarkable." Tobi was suddenly fighting back tears of joy and every bit of nervousness she'd been battling about tonight seemed to simply evaporate into a fine mist. The fact they had gone to so much effort to make sure everything was perfect, humbled her and she felt her love for them growing with each moment.

"Well, we had a bit of help, but we've sent Gracie and her men on their way." Kent's words were whispered right against her ear and sent a shiver of desire all the way to her core. "And I want you to know, love, it was worth every rushed moment to see the look of appreciation on your sweet face."

Stopping at the foot of the bed, she moved so she faced them both. "I cannot begin to tell you how much I love it or how much it means to me that you went to all the trouble to make tonight so incredibly special. I was nervous…even though I've already been staying here and this isn't our first time…" She had to take a deep breath before she could continue because she was determined that she wasn't going to cry. "But tonight, well…this marks the official beginning of our lives together…and…"

KENT HAD TRIED to let their sweet wife finish speaking, but she was teetering on the edge of her control despite her determination to hold it together. Not wanting her to feel as though she'd failed, he stepped forward and pulled her against his chest. "You are absolutely right, love. This is the beginning of our lives together and we wanted to start it right."

"Kitten, we're no different than any other men and we've made some mistakes along the way. However, we want to fill your life with beautiful memories—starting right now. We're looking forward to sitting on the porch of the home we'll build soon and listen to you tell our grandchildren how loved you felt on your wedding night. Our grandsons will need the role models and our granddaughters will learn the importance of choosing men who love them enough to make their memories just as sweet." Kyle had always insisted Kent was the charmer, but ever since Tobi had entered their lives, Kent had noticed a very significant change in his brother.

While Kyle had been painting that picture in her mind, Kent had stepped behind Tobi and was running his hands from her wrists up to her soft shoulders. Leaning over, he pressed his lips against the soft skin behind her ear and felt her relax into his touch. She was so incredibly sensual and he loved how she reacted to both he and his brother with equal passion. "Gracie's gift is lovely, but it has to go before one of us rips it off of you, love." Kent slid the straps over her gently sloping shoulders and watched as the supple fabric of her gown skimmed down her body like soft rippling water to puddle around her tiny bare feet. He watched his brother step closer to Tobi and lifted her breasts in his large hands, leaning down to suck first one nipple and then the other causing her to arch toward the touch, and the movement pressed her tighter against Kent's chest. "You are so responsive, love. And that is a gift you give to us, and one we'll always treasure."

Kent was convinced she would be able to fully embrace her submissive nature once she understood what she would gain from the power exchange. Tobi had been taking care of herself for a very long time and suddenly having two Dominant husbands who not only *wanted* to take care of her, but would insist on it, was sure to cause some power struggles. He'd seen enough fireworks between his parents over the years to know that their sweet wife would challenge them forever—or at least he sure hoped she would. He planned to make sure paddling her sweet little perfectly padded ass was a pleasure for both of them—and "make-up sex" with Tobi would be phenomenal. There would be plenty of time to help Tobi discover all the benefits a D/s lifestyle could offer her—*later*.

Kent smiled at Tobi's wide-eyed look of surprise when she realized they had actually been moving her while she'd been lost in a haze of desire. He hoped they could continue to keep her off-center enough she would only remember the pleasures they had planned for her rather than her fear or the first bites of pain that were inevitable. After laying her back in the middle of their over-sized bed, Kyle positioned himself at her side while Kent knelt between her spread legs. "Bend your knees and move your feet as far apart as you can." He didn't touch her or watch as she complied with his order, instead he kept his eyes focused on hers. Watching her pupils dilate until only a sliver of dark green encircled them was more erotic than anything he could ever remember seeing. Knowing the desire reflected in her expression was radiating up from her soul was intoxicating in its allure. "You are pure perfection, love."

Lowering himself so his mouth was close enough to her pussy that he could feel the heat of her body against his lips, he snaked the tip of his tongue out and ran it around the outside of her clit as it began to peek out from beneath its protective hood. When her entire body arched in a reaction that was pure reflex, Kent watched as Kyle splayed his large hand over her abdomen and pushed her gently back to the bed. "Stay put, kitten, or we'll have to move to the playroom so we can properly restrain you. That isn't where we want to spend our wedding night. Soon—very, very soon—it is going to be imperative that you control your movements. We don't want you to tear the tender tissues we plan on lighting up like the Fourth of July." Kent smiled to himself because he knew she didn't have a prayer of holding still when they began the full-court press that would jack her pleasure so high her movements would become purely instinctual. But he also knew Kyle's words would give them some measure of control at that time because Tobi's true nature as a submissive would compel her to follow their commands even when her body was screaming at her to vault itself over the canyon's ledge into bliss.

Kent continued his oral onslaught and pressed his fingers against the insides of the very tops of Tobi's thighs where he could feel her pulse beating wildly as she began panting, "Oh my God in heaven. I just don't...I don't know any words...that can—" That was the last words she managed before Kent felt her body begin to shudder against his touch as her release exploded, sending a wave of her sweet cream over his tongue and he lapped it eagerly. She'd screamed his name out as she had come and Kent tried not to gloat over that fact.

"You taste so fucking good, my sweet wife. I could stay right here for the rest of the night, but we have bigger things planned for you, love." He'd spoken against her sensitive tissues and knew the vibration of his words would extend her pleasure. Kent grinned up at Kyle who was watching Tobi with a stunned expression of pure reverence on his face. Kyle looked like he'd just seen a woman come for the first time and there was a very large part of Kent that understood exactly what his brother was feeling.

Chapter Twenty-Three

TOBI WASN'T SURE she was going to survive her wedding night. The orgasm she'd just experienced had nearly leveled her and Kent hadn't done anything but encircle her clit with his tongue and caress each fold with his very talented tongue. "I don't understand" was all she'd managed to utter before Kyle had leaned over her and pressed his lips to hers for a sweetly chaste kiss.

"You don't understand how you came so quickly? Or without feeling one of us inside your sweet body? Or why the feelings seem to be magnified? Are those the questions bubbling their way to the surface, kitten?" Tobi was momentarily stunned into silence because he'd just described her emotions perfectly when she hadn't even understood them herself.

"Yes. That is exactly it. How did you know?"

"Sweetheart, it was written all over your beautiful face. The emotional bond we all share intensifies the pleasure and I'm overjoyed that you have already noticed its effect." Tobi knew she was staring at him with what surely must look like a blank expression, but in fact she was trying very hard to process the words he'd just spoken. On one level it made perfect sense, but there was a piece of her heart still living in fear that it was simply too good to be true.

Tobi girl, if you let them mold you...you hand over your soul to these men...and what will you have in the end?

"You'll have everything, kitten. And yes you asked that out loud. We fell in love with you just as you are, so why would we want to change you?"

It was as if a light had suddenly been turned on inside of her and the flood of awareness was shocking. She heard Kent's soft laughter and realized he moved up along her other side. "I'd say she just *got it,* brother." He used his fingers to move her chin so her attention was focused on his face. "Did you just have an epiphany, love? Because the realization just played over your face like one of those animated billboard signs."

Tobi giggled at the picture Kent's words had put in her mind and Kyle took advantage of her moment of distraction by pulling her onto his chest. "Well, now that you seem to be back on a more even keel, I think it's time for us to upset the apple cart again." Positioning her so her drenched pussy lips were gliding along the length of his engorged cock, they both groaned at the sensation. "Jesus, Joseph, and Mary. You are so wet and if the outer lips of your pussy are this hot, you're going to burn me up when I sink into you, aren't you, kitten?"

She needed him inside her...*Now!* And she didn't doubt for a second that she was going to pay dearly for it, but she didn't care about the consequences. Reaching her hand between their bodies, she wrapped her hand around him and her inner child was suddenly happy dancing like a court jester because her fingers didn't meet and he was all hers. *Mine...my husband....my love....my Master.* She didn't give him a chance to react to her touch before pushing down over him so the smooth glans hooding his cock was inside, and then she sat up and pressed back so he slid in deep. She didn't stop until the slit at his tip was pressing kisses against her cervix and she rocked back and forth twice before he stilled her movements with a vise-like grip on her hips.

"*Fuck!* Kitten, stop. I want this to last and you are going to push me over in record time like that." Tobi didn't want to push Kyle over the edge and she really hadn't intended to go as far as she had gone, but she'd been so lost in the pleasure she hadn't been thinking clearly. She tried to pull back her own release, but the tremors in her core wouldn't still and within seconds her head fell back as she screamed out Kyle's name. Somewhere in the fog rolling through her muddled brain Tobi realized Kyle had pulled her against his chest, his kiss had a feeling of urgency that told her how close he was to losing his own control. As the kiss ended and she tried to draw in deep, gasping breaths, she felt cool lube dribble over her rear hole just before Kent's finger began massaging the outer ring of muscles. Her entire body stiffened at the intimacy.

"Don't tense up, kitten. Relax into his touch. Let that first pinch of pain wash through you as it melts into pleasure." Tobi made a conscious effort to relax and settle herself around Kyle's words as Kent's fingers began working their magic and suddenly her desire was once again racing upward. One finger was replaced by two, and when Kent withdrew from her, she heard herself moan at the feeling of emptiness.

At the first touch of the smooth head of Kent's cock pressing incessantly against her rear star, Tobi felt her body begin pushing back onto him as she heard him say, "Hold her, brother." Kyle quickly banded his muscular arms around her back and she knew she wasn't going to be able to move until they allowed it.

Knowing they were now in complete control of her pleasure was oddly liberating and Tobi felt her body start to drift deeper into the sublime pleasure. The burn of her stretching tissues was just on the verge of pulling her back to the moment when she felt the tortured outer ring relax as Kent's corona pushed through. "Love, you are so fucking tight. You are squeezing me like a tight fist and I'm skating along a very fine edge here, sweetness, so just let us do all the work—*please*."

Tobi was much too lost in everything she was feeling to have any hope of controlling even the smallest response. She felt as if she was floating as Kent pushed all the way in and when he groaned a very colorful litany of curses against her ear she couldn't even manage to smile.

Kyle's voice whispered against her other ear, "Kitten, there are no words to describe what I'm feeling. Knowing you have entrusted us with your body in this way is totally intoxicating. The only thing we need from you right now is your pleasure."

After his words, she felt Kyle lift her until the head of his cock was barely inside her and then as he pushed back in, Kent withdrew. They continued their alternating pace until she worried she was going to lose her mind to the intense pleasure sweeping though her. She hadn't even known the earth shattering release was upon her until she felt it crash over her in a pounding, cresting tsunami force wave. There were flashing lights behind her eyelids and she heard a hoarse scream rent the air and then there was nothing but blessed silence in the dark void she'd tumbled into.

KENT HAD KNOWN the first time he and his brother took Tobi together it was going to be special, but he hadn't been prepared for the intensity of the emotional bonding that had taken place. An arc of pure electricity had fused their souls together and he'd been left trying to hold himself up on arms that were trembling from the most humbling moment of his entire life.

"She's done. We need to move her and clean her up while she's out." Kent heard Kyle's words but it took several seconds before he could assign meaning to what his brother had said and several more seconds before he could actually move. Finally pushing himself off and then pulling out of her sweet body would have revived his libido if the rest of his muscles hadn't been rioting in protest.

After they'd cleaned Tobi they'd heard her soft, even breaths and knew she was sleeping soundly. They had both marveled at how soundly she slept when they were near and how quickly she seemed to wake if they left the room. After cleaning themselves up, they blew out the candles and then settled alongside her. Kyle chuckled when Tobi immediately started scooting toward him. "She's like a little heat seeking missile."

Kent knew exactly what his brother was referring to, because Tobi would snuggle up so close that she was almost a blanket around whomever she was facing. And if the other man didn't press against her back in short order, she'd come awake and start looking around with that adorable dazed expression they both loved so much. "We need to get some rest. Our flight is early and I want to leave early enough that we don't have to worry about missing it." Kyle agreed.

They had managed to convince Tobi that they were waiting a few months before taking a honeymoon trip. It had been easy since she knew how anxious they were to get the forum shops opened. They had worked with their parents' travel agent to plan a three-week trip that would start in the Greek Isles and end in Thailand. During their military service, they had been assigned to some unimaginable places, but they'd also seen some of the best the world had to offer. The locations they had chosen offered history as well as some of the most spectacular scenery in the world and they were looking forward to sharing it all with the woman who had literally come out of a storm and stolen their hearts.

Epilogue

Three months later

GRACIE SANTOS LOVED her new job. Working as the assistant manager for The Forum Shops at the Prairie Winds Club was a dream come true. After her best friend and boss, Tobi, and her two husbands returned from their honeymoon, it had been a full-on push to get the small shops stocked, the displays put together, and all the advance notifications sent out to the club's growing list of members. Gracie had found herself struggling to overcome her embarrassment each time she'd opened a box and helped with displays of dildos and a variety of other "toys." She and Tobi had ended up on the floor in fits of giggles more than once as they'd tried to imagine what some of the items were supposed to be used for.

While Tobi, Kyle, and Kent West had been on their honeymoon trip, Micah Drake and Jax McDonald had moved her into the small guest cabin at the back of the Prairie Winds property. All three Wests had apologized because it was the smallest of their cabins, but in Gracie's opinion, it was perfect. The front porch ran the length of the one bedroom structure and had a comfortable patio set where she often relaxed with her morning coffee. The kitchenette was tiny but had everything she could want including a microwave that worked and that was far better than the apartment she'd been forced to vacate when the building had been sold.

Everything in the little guest house was clean and updated, and the only time it felt small was when Jax or Micah were there. Both men were big, but at six foot eleven, Jax made even the largest room seem small. Smiling to herself as she shelved the last items from another box of new merchandise, she heard the voices of men as they approached the shop she was working in. Gracie grabbed up the empty cardboard box and made her way around the corner into the back room. The Wests had given numerous tours of the shops during the past month and she wanted the small space to look pristine when they entered.

Just as she was ready to round the corner to reenter the shop she recognized a voice she had hoped she would never hear again. The voice of a man who had promised her the sun and the moon, but had delivered hell on earth. The voice of a man who she'd barely managed to escape once. Backing slowly to the rear exit of the small shop, Gracie managed to open the door without making even a whisper of sound. As soon as she was outside, she tried to calm her racing heart because she knew fear wouldn't help her escape.

Turning to make a run back to her small cabin to pack, Gracie ran directly into a rock solid chest. She screamed and instinct kicked in as she fought to escape. And just as the darkness was closing in around her, she heard Micah Drake's voice, "Gracie? What the hell? *Stop!*" but it was too late, she had already let the darkness take her.

The End

Books by Avery Gale

The Wolf Pack Series
Mated – Book One
Fated Magic – Book Two
Tempted by Darkness – Book Three

Masters of the Prairie Winds Club
Out of the Storm
Saving Grace
Jen's Journey
Bound Treasure
Punishing for Pleasure
Accidental Trifecta
Missionary Position

The ShadowDance Club
Katarina's Return – Book One
Jenna's Submission – Book Two
Rissa's Recovery – Book Three
Trace & Tori – Book Four
Reborn as Bree – Book Five
Red Clouds Dancing – Book Six
Perfect Picture – Book Seven

Club Isola

Capturing Callie – Book One

Healing Holly – Book Two

Claiming Abby – Book Three

I would love to hear from you!

Email:

avery.gale@ymail.com

Website:

www.averygalebooks.com/index.html

Facebook:

facebook.com/avery.gale.3

Instagram:

avery.gale

Twitter:

@avery_gale

Excerpt from Mated

The Wolf Pack
Book One
by Avery Gale

Jameson Wolf had been almost ready to head home when he'd taken one last look out of the front windows of his office. Looking down over the sidewalk below, he wondered why the waiting line was so long on a frigid Friday night. He'd started to turn back to the room when his eye caught on a flash of red. Damn it to hell, he'd always had a thing for auburn haired women. Redheads were rare among shifters so he took a closer look. It might have been her long flowing mane of red curls that caught his attention, but there was something about her saucy attitude that drew him in. Watching her, he saw her easy rapport with the tiny blonde beauty she was with and he liked the fact that she seemed oblivious to the fact that she turned the head of every man near her.

Making his way down the steep circular staircase he was assailed by the overpowering scents of both humans and his peers who had braved the biting cold January night in the wind swept city. He saw the red-haired beauty enter through the heavy doorway a split second before the scent of his mate barreled over him. It was as if every neuron in his brain had been suddenly struck by lightning and was now crackling with electrical energy. His vision tunneled and his sole mission became to find the owner of that scent and mark her as his.

As he neared the red-haired beauty who had caught his eye earlier, the exotic fragrance he'd been following became more and more potent. *Could I actually be that lucky after all these years?* Stepping up behind her he took a deep breath letting her scent soak deeply into his soul. Even though he loved the fresh citrus smell of her hair, it was the essence of her that was nearly over-powering in its allure. It pulled him in and made every one of his senses come sharply into a pinpoint focus. He'd heard his friends describe this moment, but he had truly believed that their words had been little more than romantic folly—until now.

When she turned toward him, he became instantly aware that she'd been planning to escape. There was a look of panic in her eyes—what he didn't understand was what had spooked her. Awareness and anxiety were coming off her in heavy, crashing waves. He could smell fear in humans and shifters, but that wasn't what he was picking up. No, she wasn't afraid of him, but she wasn't thrilled to have been found either. *Interesting.* Mating scents are an almost overwhelmingly powerful draw for both male and female shifters so there was no doubt she had known her mate was near. So why was she trying to leave?

Both Jameson and his brother, Trevlon, were the Alphas of their pack and had been since their fathers were killed by rivals seven years ago. They had always known they'd follow pack tradition and share a mate, but they hadn't had any luck finding her despite having traveled all over the globe searching. *How has this beauty flown under our radar? She is exactly the type of woman we are both attracted to.*

"What is your name, beautiful?" Jameson knew his words had come out as more of a growl than a question, but considering how close he was to claiming her right here in the middle of the club, it was the best he could do. He relaxed a bit when he saw her deer in the headlights look. *Good – I'm happy to know she is as slammed by the attraction as I am.*

"Kit." He heard the wobble of nervousness in her voice and could tell she had barely been able to squeak out the word so he just waited. He saw her draw in a deep breath through her mouth and almost laughed at her ineffective attempt to avoid breathing through her nose. He tried to suppress his smile when she repeated the gesture because it was a futile attempt to escape the scent of her mate.

Once a shifter found their mate, their bodies were taken over by overwhelming sexual urges that lasted for weeks. He'd seen pack members all but disappear during that time because they could barely leave their bedrooms. He waited patiently as she finally seemed to come back to awareness and answered, "I mean, Kathleen, my name is Kathleen Harris." She was trying to look around him, which was amusing because she couldn't be more than five feet three or four inches tall and that was including the ridiculously high-heeled black leather stiletto boots she was wearing.

He was sure she hadn't meant to give him her nickname because it was likely something she reserved for those she considered close friends, so when he addressed her again, he used it deliberately. "Well, Kit, follow me, please."

He turned on his heel and started back toward the staircase when she reached out and grasped his forearm. "Wait, I can't go with you. I don't even know you. And my friend will be looking for me." The instant she touched him he'd felt a jolt of electricity arc between them and then tiny bolts of lightning streaked up his spine. *Damn, her touch did that through the fabric of his shirt, what would it feel like when they were skin to skin?*

The twin bond between him and Trev had always been incredibly strong, so he wasn't at all surprised when his phone rang. "Where are you? Are you okay?" Typical Trevlon, straight to it—he couldn't be troubled to utter a polite greeting.

"Standing in front of a woman I want you to meet. We're in the bar, but we'll be on our way upstairs as soon as we locate her friend to let her know where we are heading. Meet us in the office in five." Jameson disconnected the call and turned to one of his staff that was walking by. He quickly gave the man a detailed description of Kit's friend and instructions to stay close to her and keep her safe until she was ready to leave the building. At that time, he was to accompany her to the office. Jameson stood six foot seven inches tall in his boots, so he could easily see the tiny blonde on the other side dance floor and directed the young man to her. Jameson was glad it had been Charlie who'd been the first to walk by. He trusted the young shifter to do exactly as he'd been told.

Turning back to Kit, he realized for the first time that he had taken the hand she'd used to grab his arm and was holding it in his own. He'd been rubbing small circles over the inside of her wrist with his thumb. As his gaze met hers he felt her pulse speed up and watched as her pupils dilated. "Come along, Kit. We need to talk." This time he did smell fear so he pulled her into his arms and leaned down so his words would be painted over the soft shell of her ear like a warm brush of air, "I won't hurt you—ever. Be brave, sweet kitten."

Made in the USA
Columbia, SC
03 July 2017